Soul Riders

JORVIK CALLING

HELENA DAHLGREN

TRANSLATION BY
AGNES BROOMÉ

Andrews McMeel
PUBLISHING®

The Great
Reservoir

CRATER OF JOR

Ashland

Valley of the
idden Dinosaur

NORTHSHIRE

CENTRAL JORVIK

Firgrove
Village

GROVE

Jorvik City

uth Link

MISTFALL

Dundull

RN JORVIK

Sometimes life forces you to make a decision that will change the future forever.

It is true that you choose your own path in life. You shape your own destiny. But sometimes, fate chooses for you.

Legend speaks of a girl on horseback who will save the world. Her light and wisdom will dispel the darkness and chaos. She will put everything right.

Are you the one?

Prologue

Once upon a time, in the Cold Sea, lay a lifeless isle where darkness reigned.

One day, a star fell from the sky, and out of its strong, flaming glow came a girl on horseback. As she rode slowly across the sea, her horse's hooves tamed the wild waves beneath her. In her right hand, she held the light of life; in her left, a golden harp. The music of the harp awoke the surrounding nature. She lay the light down on the island, and life and hope poured out of the cold nothingness. Warmth and brightness spread over everything that had been dead. Everything was new. But the girl's spirit could not endure. She dissolved into nature, into the winds, the rain, the teardrops of the dew. Some claim she remains there to this day. Listen, and you might hear her in the wondrously clear song of the birds, or feel her in the soft caress of the breeze on a warm summer's day.

As the island called Jorvik came into being, good and evil entered the world.

Light cannot exist without darkness, as darkness cannot exist without light. The struggle between good and evil has been secretly raging for thousands of years. A great darkness hides in the depths of the ocean, biding its time, waiting just a little while longer.

Jorvik, located somewhere between Norway, Iceland, and the British Isles, of which it was once part, is a nexus of worlds.

Horse people come to experience the island's equestrian culture and abundance of horse breeds, and nature lovers seek it out to admire Jorvik's natural beauty. However, it's also sought out by companies that want to ruthlessly exploit its precious natural resources. A small number of these visitors hold Jorvik's fate in their hands, but most do not. Many who have been to Jorvik before seem to have forgotten that the island exists, the same way a dream fades into nothing when you wake up in the morning. If you hear about Jorvik, the name will soon escape you again. It's as though the island is a myth. "That island again . . . Somewhere in Scandinavia, right? Iceland?"

Dark days await beautiful Jorvik. Evil is poised to be unleashed. Should that come to pass, everything will be lost. Yet while the raging sea seethes and hisses, hope lives, for it is taking root in the secret order of druids who are dedicated to standing against this doomsday scenario. The foremost champions of these druids are called the Soul Riders.

The Soul Riders are chosen girls who share a special bond with their horses. Through that bond, they acquire special powers to help them in their fight against evil. It has been many years since the Soul Riders defended Jorvik, but there are rumors that the time has come for a new sisterhood to form.

1

"Are we there yet?"

Lisa was fifteen years old, but she felt like a squirmy, impatient five-year-old as she asked the same question for the tenth time since they'd gotten in the van. How long had they been waiting, ten minutes?

Her dad just smiled and lightly drummed his fingers against the steering wheel.

"They should be letting us off the ferry any minute now, Isa," he replied. "They already started unloading."

"It feels like we've been sitting here for hours," Lisa muttered. She couldn't help but flinch at the sound of her old nickname. It made her think of a determined little girl with disheveled red hair. Plump cheeks and a T-shirt with a horse motif. Always horses. Always on her way somewhere, following her mom or dad or the mild-mannered family cat who used to sleep curled up in a ball by her feet. Isa *is the photo album version of Lisa Peterson*, she thought to herself. The past. History. She doesn't have much in common with the here-and-now Lisa who was sitting in the passenger seat of an old van, waiting for her new life to start.

Again.

She noticed that a whiny tone had crept into her voice. No wonder, considering the fact that she'd spent all night twisting and turning in the uncomfortable bunk bed pressed against the wall of their small cabin. Her dad, Carl, had insisted that they "splurge" on the cabin for their overnight journey on the ferry. He had fallen asleep instantly. She had lain awake, feeling the waves billowing beneath her, trying to block out the sound of her dad's snoring.

She barely slept a wink. She could feel it in her head, which was heavy and foggy. Everything was blurred, somewhere between wakefulness and sleeping, as though all she'd have to do to touch the previous night's hazy dreams was reach out her hand.

Clattering hooves. A canter that turned into a frenzied gallop. A terrified scream—hers? And then sheer silence. Darkness. She blinked hard, trying to push the nightmarish images away.

Her dad smiled and reached over to stroke her hair.

"Just wait until we get off this ferry. I know I've shown you pictures of the island, but you'll get a better idea of what it's like when you see it for yourself. It's unlike any place you've ever seen."

Lisa reluctantly returned his smile and wondered how her dad could be so excited about anything at six o'clock in the morning.

She had, of course, seen pictures of Jorvik. High mountains, gently rolling hills, and a rich shade of green that almost looked photoshopped. The vast blue sea around the island seemed endless. It brought to mind the colorful fairy tales she'd read when she was little. The only thing missing was the rainbow.

She tried to imagine herself in a place like that, one of those fantastical lands. Regular old Lisa in her worn-out jeans and an old hoodie, with her headphones around her neck or resting snugly over her tousled, bright-red hair. But the image wouldn't come.

They were in a rented van full of moving boxes, waiting for the man on the PA system, having just cheerfully welcomed them to Jorvik, to tell them it was okay to start their engines. Lisa pulled her headphones over her ears and disappeared into one of her favorite songs. That usually helped, but not this morning.

After a second, she gave up, pulling her headphones off again and staring straight ahead at the caravan of cars and trucks that were slowly starting to move down the ramp.

They'd been traveling for the better part of two days, first by van and then by ferry. And now they'd finally arrived in Jorvik. Their new home. Lisa's dad had accepted a job on one of the island's largest oil platforms and Lisa was due to start school on Monday. She didn't quite know what to expect. What did this island, this *Jorvik*, which her dad hadn't been able to stop talking about, really have to offer aside from a massive oil platform, picturesque surroundings, and lots of horses?

There was a time when Lisa lived for horses, when the thought of living on an island like Jorvik, a place where horses seemed central to everything, would have been a dream come true. However, when Lisa was twelve, her mother was suddenly killed in a riding accident. Grief clawed at her like a ravenous wolf whenever she let herself think about it, so she tried her best not to.

In the three years since the accident, she hadn't so much as looked at a horse. All the posters, books, clothes, and films—anything that reminded her of that day—were put into boxes, taped up, and taken away. Her riding gear had been donated to charity. Lisa was never going to ride again. The mere thought of it was too painful.

We have a girl here. She's in shock but conscious, no visible injuries. A woman dead at the scene.

The darkness, the pitch-black despair, could open up any time. Anywhere.

Her dad turned on the radio and an upbeat Madonna song from the 1980s filled the van. They both started singing along, but then looked at each other and exchanged bittersweet smiles that didn't quite reach their eyes. This was Lisa's mom's favorite song. They both knew this but didn't say anything. There was no need. The pain echoed through the van, all the way to the back, where a framed photograph of her mom was wrapped carefully in a T-shirt and packed away in one of the boxes.

A faded photograph in a box was all that was left. Lisa felt like she was never going to be able to accept her death.

Sometimes she feared she might be starting to forget her mom. Those small, everyday details that she had the luxury of taking for granted for twelve years. Like all children do.

She had noticed that the details of her mother had slowly started to fade from her mind. She felt lucky that she had music to help her remember. Two beats of this old Madonna song and her mom was right there, so clearly, dancing in the kitchen with a spatula in one hand and Lisa's hand gripped tightly in the other, the sun streaming in through the windows.

But as the song finished, another memory surfaced. Her mom riding ahead of Lisa, racing up a hill in Texas, just moments before the accident. Then how her shallow, gasping breaths filled the void next to Lisa's heavy ones. The bottomless darkness became overwhelming as her breathing slowed. Her rapid, faint heartbeats were similar to a sick animal. Her cheek was still soft and warm against Lisa's when the ambulance had arrived. The next time she saw her mother was in the hospital. By then, her cheek was cold. Waxy, like that of a doll.

Lisa quickly blinked away her tears. She looked out the side window so her dad wouldn't see.

Don't think about Mom.

Don't think about horses . . . .

What should I think about?

No, Lisa wasn't exactly looking forward to moving to Jorvik. She knew no one, *was* no one. Starting from scratch. But she'd have to make it work, she thought to herself.

It wasn't like she hadn't been the new girl before. Her dad's jobs on various oil platforms had taken her from Texas to Norway to Alaska, back to Norway, and now to Jorvik. Always the new girl in class, never entirely at home. Never entirely part of the group.

She was used to the struggle of learning everything all over again: the names of her classmates, all the unspoken codes and rules. Sometimes, Lisa felt homeless. Rootless.

For a few years, horses had been her escape. Since the accident, music had taken their place. Lisa was always singing, even when she wasn't aware of it.

Maybe particularly in these moments. She loved music. All kinds of music, old and new. Granted, she preferred country and rock to her mom's more pop-oriented tastes.

Still, she couldn't help singing along to the Madonna song. It helped her remember.

She still had all her mom's old CDs. They were in one of the boxes in the back of the van. The playlist she was just listening to was full of her mom's favorite songs. What would she have thought of this move? What would she think about Jorvik?

I thought I told you not to think about Mom.

Lisa jumped when her dad suddenly honked angrily at the car in front of them.

"Hey, move it along! We're getting off now!" He pressed his hand down even harder on the horn. "I have to find somewhere that sells coffee," he mumbled. He had only had time for one watery cup of coffee during their quick breakfast on board.

"Um, Dad? I'm pretty sure he can't hear you," Lisa murmured.

She was unable to hide her sulkiness, but something gentle and light had slipped into her voice, making her dad's eyes well up when he thought she wasn't looking.

But Lisa noticed. She was, in fact, happy to be sitting there with her dad. They only had each other. It was the two of them, forever.

Finally, it was their turn to roll off the ferry. They drove straight into a landscape that was like nothing Lisa had ever seen before. She couldn't help gasping as she took in the dark, majestic firs blanketing the rolling green hills and the sides of the towering mountains.

The landscape was somewhat similar to Norway's, Lisa thought. However, it was even vaster and wilder, as if Jorvik's colors had all been magnified by a Technicolor filter. Lisa began to wonder whether she had ever truly seen real colors before. It felt like she hadn't. The sun was slowly rising, but the pale crescent of the moon was still visible among the deeply lavender sky.

One star fell as an array of new ones seemed to twinkle to life. Lisa frowned. That was odd; wasn't the sun just about to come up?

She opened her window and stuck her head out. She breathed in the distinct smell she would later think of as the Jorvik smell, a mix of salt, soil, and something almost sweet.

It was neither day nor night but something in between. Apart from the other passengers slowly making their way off of the large ferry, Lisa and her dad were all alone in a city that was just waking up.

Jorvik. Maybe she could live here after all.

2

"Look at the sky, Dad!"

For the first time since they set off for Jorvik, Lisa sounded happy. Excited, almost. Her dad yawned and mumbled something inaudible from behind the wheel. Lisa shook her head and turned back to look out the window.

What was happening in the sky? Whatever it was, was the coolest thing she'd ever seen. She could count more hues and shades than in the box of watercolors her mom had given her for Christmas many years ago. Shades of red, purple, pink, and gold gleamed and glittered, like a giant rainbow blanketed the sky and stretched out over the sea.

It was barely morning, but the night stars continued to twinkle. Despite the darkness, they were so clear and bright they almost looked fake. It seemed to Lisa that they were all twinkling to the rhythm of her heartbeat.

Still no sound came from the driver's seat. Lisa took a deep breath and tried again, a little louder this time: "The sky, Dad! Is that the Northern Lights or what? Look at all the stars—I had no idea they could be that bright! Did you? Do you see how they form a giant star? Dad, come on, look!"

"Mm-hmm . . . ," her dad mumbled.

He was completely engrossed in the map that was supposed to guide them to the small town of Jarlaheim. Their new home was located just outside the center of town.

Eventually they passed through the gates of Jarlaheim's massive, medieval, city wall and stopped in the middle of a square. The square was completely quiet and deserted.

Pretty cozy, Lisa mused. She stared down one of the cobbled streets that led away from the square and spotted several little restaurants and cafés.

She could picture herself sitting in one of them on a sunny fall day with a big cup of tea and a fancy dessert. Talking to her dad, or maybe—she took a deep breath and dared to consider the thought—some new friends.

Her dad scanned the area for somewhere to buy coffee and accidentally put his arm on the horn, making it honk loudly.

"How is this possible?" he screamed. "Not a single place open! I need coffee!"

Her dad drove on, out through another stone gate in the city wall. Lisa studied him and thought about the jar of instant coffee she had packed as a backup in case the new house didn't have a coffee machine. She knew what her dad was like when he didn't get his caffeine. Lisa smiled to herself and turned her eyes back to the colorful, morning sky.

Just above one of the mountain tops, the giant star-shaped constellation was still shining so brightly that it was almost blinding. It wasn't the Big Dipper or any of the other constellations her mom and dad had pointed out to her when she was little.

No, this was something else. Lisa had never seen anything like it before.

High above their van, the stars traced the outline of a large, four-pointed star in the paling morning sky. She turned back to her dad. *He hasn't noticed any of it,* she thought to herself. *How is that even possible?*

The sunrise eventually chased the strange four-pointed star from the sky. In the soft morning light, the first fall leaves shimmered on the trees like spun gold. Lisa's dad drove on toward their new home.

In the center of the sleepy town, a drowsy girl with long, jet-black hair pulled back into a messy bun opened the front door of a limestone house. She took off her large glasses and rubbed her eyes, still blurry with sleep. As she looked into the small, neat garden, she noted the roses were still in full bloom. While this might be unusual elsewhere in fall, it was normal for Jorvik. One of the things she loved about living there was how everything seemed to obey different laws. Even something as fundamental as nature couldn't be predicted or tamed.

"Would you fetch the paper please, Linda?" a voice called out.

"I'm already on my way, Aunt Amal!"

Linda slipped her feet into a pair of clogs and pulled one of her aunt's coats over her nightgown for the short trip to the mailbox. Her little black cat bolted out the door, rubbed itself against her legs, and proceeded to meow loudly.

"What's the matter, Misty?" Linda asked sleepily, scratching the cat behind its one intact ear.

The air was cool on this September morning. The cat's eyes were big and green, and they reflected a bright light coming from somewhere in the sky.

Linda picked up the cat and then looked up.

Her eyes were fixed on the early morning sky. Right next to the fading moon, a strange constellation of stars was twinkling in the shape of a huge crescent moon. A few years ago, Linda went through a phase when she was obsessed with astronomy. She tried to learn all of the constellations by heart. She had even received a telescope for Christmas. But she had never seen this strange constellation before.

"Weird," she muttered. She glanced back down at Misty in her arms, and then walked the rest of the way to the mailbox to fetch the newspaper.

Outside a large house, in the Jorvik City area that the locals called Millionaires' Row, a pink car was parked with its engine running. A young girl dressed in riding gear, with her blond hair pulled back into a hairnet-covered bun, dashed outside. She was tall and lanky, and walked slightly bent over as if she hadn't quite grown accustomed to her height yet. The vast courtyard was flooded with harsh lights. Looking down, she noticed a tiny smudge, probably a grass stain, on her riding pants. "Shoot," she muttered under her breath. "Good thing Mom didn't notice it at breakfast."

Her mom's voice echoed from the hallway, "Have a good day at the stable, Anne! I know you're going to win this competition. You always do!"

"See you later," Anne called back as she rushed to the car.

She opened the door to the car that was going to take her to Jorvik Stables outside Jarlaheim. But before she could climb into the car, something caught her eye and she stopped abruptly. She squinted up at the sky then took a step back, blinded by what she saw.

A bright light was dancing across the sky. The last stars lingering in the early morning sky formed a constellation that looked like a giant sun.

"Weird," she mumbled. "The sun isn't even up yet."

"Come on Tin-Can! Give it all you've got!"

The girl asking for a canter had messy, tawny hair and an open, lively face that brimmed with curiosity and mischief. Her bright brown eyes matched the color of the horse she was riding. Together they flew down the forest road. It was so early that even the birds were barely awake, but Alex had come to cherish these brutally early rides on Tin-Can, her best friend and constant companion. At this hour, they had nature all to themselves.

The trails were all theirs, as was the dark forest with all its secrets, and the clearing where she often saw rabbits hopping around. Even the road back to the stables was usually quiet and deserted.

Alex liked to go fast and was never in the habit of slowing down. She liked to say that it was both a gift and a curse, and her teachers all agreed. Still, just a moment ago she and Tin-Can were standing motionless. The sky was on fire, twinkling so brightly she had to stop and look.

She saw a bright constellation shaped like an angular lightning bolt. It was a spectacular sight. She suddenly thought of her neglected Instagram page, but before she had time to take out her phone to snap a photo, the stars faded into the pale light of dawn.

Alex Cloudmill had lived on Jorvik all of her life. It was the only place on Earth she could ever imagine herself being. She almost felt sorry for all the people who had never experienced the beautiful island she called home. Especially on mornings like this one.

She pushed herself forward in the saddle and steered Tin-Can toward a ditch. They could clear it effortlessly and continue swiftly through the trees, racing toward the road that would lead them back to the stables where mucking out stalls, feeding, and grooming awaited.

They didn't see the van until it was almost too late.

Lisa and her dad were just reaching the top of a long incline when a horse and rider suddenly came bursting out of the trees at a raging gallop. Her dad slammed on the brakes and the van screeched to a halt.

The horse, a small, muscular golden chestnut with a long, wild mane reared up and nearly brought his front hooves down on the hood of their van. Lisa just about stopped breathing.

In all the commotion, a saddlebag flew free from the horse's back and landed on the ground beside the van.

Both Lisa and her dad rushed out of the van.

"Oh my god, I'm sorry!" the rider exclaimed, softly petting her horse in an effort to calm him down. "I didn't think there would be any cars out and about this early. I hope we didn't scare you."

Lisa thought the girl looked remarkably calm for someone who had just barely avoided being run over.

"Don't worry about it," Lisa's dad replied. "But you should try to be more careful. Watch where you're going from now on."

He didn't sound angry, just worried. And the girl nodded in agreement.

"I promise. Sometimes I go too fast. My name is Alex, by the way." Her brown eyes were fixed on Lisa. "Alex Cloudmill. And this maniac," she said tenderly while patting her horse, "goes by the name of Tin-Can." Tin-Can responded by chomping away at his bit and looking like he couldn't wait to get going again.

"Lisa Peterson," Lisa said, raising her hand to pet Tin-Can.

She could feel the horse's muscles rippling under her hand and flinched, taking a step back. Alex's eyes sparkled.

"It's nice to meet you, Lisa Peterson," Alex said. "Maybe I'll see you again soon."

Lisa was about to ask which school Alex went to when Alex suddenly clicked her tongue and rode off. At that moment, Lisa noticed the saddlebag lying on the ground.

"Wait, Alex! You forgot your . . ."

She picked up the saddlebag and held it up, but Alex was already out of earshot.

". . . bag," she mumbled faintly as she watched the horse and rider, who were already halfway down the hill, disappear in the distance.

On the opposite side of the road, halfway hidden under a big tree, a rider, draped in a long, gray cloak, was sitting astride a gray horse and watched the van drive off. She urged her steed on and rode after them, but neither Lisa nor her father would see so much as a trace of her today. Not yet. She was biding her time, like all of Jorvik.

3

Later that day, the temperature in Jorvik soared. It was the warmest September day the island had experienced in a long time. There wasn't a cloud in the sky.

The perfect day to explore the island, Lisa thought.

One thing was certain: it was *not* a good day to move. Especially when your father had convinced himself that they could get by just fine without a moving crew. "We'll have everything done and dusted by ourselves in an hour or two," he'd said. *Yeah, right.* Lisa rolled her eyes. It felt like they'd been carrying stuff back and forth from the van for ages.

"Almost done," her dad said, giving Lisa an encouraging nod.

She turned around and looked out across the vast lawn that bordered an even larger meadow. When her dad triumphantly told her they would have their own house on Jorvik, she had pictured some kind of modern, wooden house. Maybe something like the terraced house that they had lived in outside of Oslo before making the move to Jorvik.

She had pictured tiny, well-kept gardens and identical houses that almost touched at the property lines. Instead, her dad drove right through the suburbs and continued down a narrow, winding, gravel road until they stopped in front of an old cottage.

The closest neighbor lived on the other side of the meadow. The house that was now theirs—Lisa couldn't quite think of it as *home* just yet—was slightly crooked, with mullioned windows, twisted vines climbing up the walls, and overlapping, cinnamon-colored shingles on the slanted roof.

"This will be good for us, don't you think?" her dad had asked as he put the key in the lock. He then stepped aside so Lisa could enter and take a look around.

Lisa took a quick look around the house without answering, and then set to work unloading the boxes and bags from the back of the van.

The mountain of boxes and carrier bags in the van had become considerably smaller a good few hours later. But carrying was becoming more difficult and the heat didn't help.

Thankfully, they had been allowed to rent the house furnished from her dad's new employer, so at least they didn't have to move any heavy furniture. The sun was shining right in Lisa's eyes, and she wished she could remember where she had packed her baseball cap. Sweat trickled down her back, gathering in little puddles inside her T-shirt.

She puffed and panted.

"How many more boxes could there be? I thought you said we didn't have a lot of stuff."

Her dad laughed. "Are you getting tired? It's just a few more, okay? I can bring in the last ones if you'd prefer to start unpacking your room. Then I figured we'd head into town for pizza? That would be nice, right?"

Lisa just nodded. She couldn't stop thinking about what had happened with the girl and her horse a few hours earlier.

She shuddered when she thought about how close the horse's flailing hooves had been. It had been years since she has been that close to a horse.

The thought made her stomach turn—and not only with fear for the horse. There was something else, too. Something that had lain dormant inside her since . . . since Mom. Maybe even since before that. This *something* was somewhere between curiosity and longing. Well, that and the mountain of fear. There should be a word for that feeling, Lisa mused.

She often found that words failed her; they were not enough. That's when she turned to music. She always managed to find a movement, a melody, or a song that matched her mood. Colors have songs. Days of the week. Even people.

She thought about which song would best describe her encounter with Alex. A movie soundtrack, maybe? Woods. Darkness. A softly clinking piano and swelling strings. Dramatic percussion whipping up a faster beat. She could feel the melody inside her now. It slowly filled her until time and space floated away. The strings morphed into a different instrument. A harp, maybe? Weird.

"Ow!" Lisa squealed when a moving box fell onto her big toe.

"I'll take that one," her dad said, grabbing the box and walking toward the stairs.

Lisa straightened up. She slowly worked her way back to the present, the hallway, the boxes. Her tender, throbbing toe. What was it she had just been thinking about?

Yes. She remembered. She needed to return that girl's saddlebag. Alex. Even though she'd promised never to set foot inside a stable again. But the saddlebag probably contained things that Alex surely needed. Keys, for instance. Lisa went to find the saddlebag and opened it. She felt like a pickpocket, rifling through the contents of the bag, but it couldn't be helped. She hoped to find more clues about who the girl with the unruly horse might be, and she wasn't disappointed.

In the bag, she found a set of keys with a keyring that had "Jorvik Stables" written on it in blue, slightly smudged ink. The key-ring was in the shape of a happy-looking horse staring at a bunch of carrots. Lisa felt like the horse was almost smirking at her.

We had barely been on this island for five minutes before a horse appeared and there was almost another accident, she thought.

And yet, something was pulling her toward Jorvik Stables. Something irresistible and mysterious. She could clearly hear the melody.

It continued to rise within her along with the strong harp notes that wouldn't subside. But she couldn't quite sing along with the lyrics yet. Suddenly she didn't care that she was sweaty, or that the bright September sun was hurting her eyes.

"Dad? How far is Jorvik Stables from here?"

"I think it's pretty close. Why don't you ride your bike over there tomorrow? I'll show you the way on the map. And you have your phone, too, in case you get lost."

"Bike?" Lisa asked, confused. She didn't have a bike.

"Didn't you see the blue bike in the driveway?" her dad replied. "It's for you. A gift from my employer. Isn't that nice?"

Lisa nodded, suddenly realizing how tired and hungry she was. How lovely it would be to sit down at the kitchen table with her father, eat pizza, and talk about what they were going to do with their new house. How they were going to make it a home and not just a place to live. And then they would talk about all the exploring they were going to do, and all the excursions they were going to go on when her dad was off work. He'd already promised that it was going to be different this time: *You're supposed to work to live, Lisa, not live to work. I need to get my bosses to remember that.*

So, the stable tomorrow. Lisa knew she was too exhausted to go anywhere today. And the shower she was about to have would be the most longed-for shower of her life.

"If it's all right, I wouldn't mind staying here when you go into town," she said. "I want to shower and unpack a bit."

"Of course," her dad replied. "I'll pick up some other supplies for the house while I'm at it."

She heard the creaking of the old hardwood floor as he walked away and then the sound of the front door closing behind him.

Lisa walked upstairs to her new room. She fiddled around randomly without doing any real unpacking. She paused, holding a framed photograph of her and her mom. Through the window she could see her father in the driveway, talking on the phone.

The bedroom was spacious, but not much bigger than her old one. The bed looked new, as though someone had just removed the plastic. It was made up with a checkered bedspread and purple and green pillows. Lisa smelled the air to see if there was a trace of perfume from whoever put so much effort into making Lisa and her father feel welcome. But she got nothing other than a hint of wood from the large desk at the far end of the room.

She wondered if that was brand new, too.

So far, only one thing revealed that the room belonged to Lisa: the nylon-stringed acoustic guitar, which she had made sure to carry in before anything else and immediately hung up over her bed. It felt important to get the guitar in place right away. She reached out and gently strummed the strings.

The room had a sterile feel to it that took her back to the hospital room three years before.

The single chair sitting next to the bed.

The white sheet that had been pulled up to her mom's chin.

These memories brought on the tears again, and this time Lisa couldn't stop them. She sat down on the bed and sobbed.

After a little while, she dried her tears and stood up. She decided she was going to have that shower now. Her legs trembled but didn't buckle. She wasn't going to be weak; that wasn't an option now.

The bathroom was sparklingly clean—almost sterile.

That won't last, she thought to herself, and smiled a little. Neither she nor her dad were particularly tidy.

Sitting on the sink was a small hand soap that looked expensive and luxurious. When she peeked behind the shower curtain, she discovered shampoo, conditioner, and shower gel. Big, fluffy towels were stacked up on the towel rack, folded just like in a hotel.

Who was her dad working for again? Did they look after all their employees this well?

She lingered in front of the bathroom mirror. The girl looking back at her looked tired. Otherwise, she was the same as always. Her disheveled red hair, the strangely shaped birthmark made up of freckles on her cheek. Since she first started to wear makeup a few years back, she'd been trying to hide it with foundation and powder. It kind of worked, but maybe she shouldn't bother. Sometimes she wondered if she should just accept that the birthmark was a part of her, just like her taste in music and love of cheap chocolate.

It had been a long time since she had allowed herself to break down like she had just then. She did feel lighter now as a result and broke her eye contact with the mirror. Lisa began to think again about all the boxes in her room. She decided the best thing would be to try to get settled in as quickly as possible. Get rid of that cold, hotel-room feeling.

Maybe Jorvik *could* be the place where she and her dad finally settled down, forgetting the past few horrible years and really starting over. This thought hit her at the same time the shower of water touched her skin. Through the open window, she heard her dad whistling in the driveway as he arrived with the pizza. She smiled and thought that she'd try, at least.

And yes, she would go over to the stables tomorrow and return the saddlebag to Alex. That's the kind of thing the new Lisa was going to do. She turned off the water and stepped out of the shower.

"Welcome to Jorvik, Lisa Peterson," she whispered.

4

During their first night in the new house, Lisa dreamt of riding a horse. She'd had the same dream before, more times than she could count. The details weren't always the same—there were little shifts in time and space—but Lisa always thought of it as "the dream." Sometimes the mood in the dream was dark. Sometimes it was light, like that night, and she wasn't afraid of riding. Fear belonged to the darkness.

Together with her horse, which was a beautiful light gray color with a long, bluish mane, she flew across green meadows and over a babbling brook. She and the horse were the perfect team. The canter was smooth and flowing. Lisa's commands were almost unnoticeable.

Lisa knew this horse well. It had been appearing in her dreams since she was a little girl.

In elementary school, she drew a blue mane and tail on all her horses. Her teachers tried to persuade her to try other colors. One even began to wonder whether Lisa might be color-blind. Surely Lisa knew that's not what *real* horses looked like? But Lisa stubbornly insisted. This particular horse *did* have a blue mane and tail. She knew it did, because that's how it had looked in her dreams.

It had been a long time since Lisa had dreamt about this horse. And yet, it still felt familiar. It felt like coming home. There was a time when she had welcomed this nightly dream. But then it turned into a nightmare after her mother's accident.

Had she come home now? Finally? Ever since she was little, Lisa had felt an inexplicable urge to be somewhere else. She didn't know much about what this other place might be. Where to find it, or if it even existed. But she knew, without understanding why, that *that* horse lived there. Could Jorvik possibly be that place?

In the dream, it was sunny. Birds were singing. The whole setting was almost too perfect.

But even so, Lisa could feel anxiety surrounding her, like a cloud suddenly invading a clear blue sky. The birds stopped singing. Darkness fell quickly, and the day was relentlessly chased away by a thick, sticky gloom.

She was suddenly aware of someone grabbing her leg. Her riding boot slipped out of her stirrup and she struggled to keep her balance. Her horse galloped faster and faster. At the same time, the grip around her leg grew firmer, tightening like a vice.

Don't look down, a voice said suddenly. *Whatever you do, don't look down.*

She couldn't help herself and looked down. She gasped when she saw the enormous black tentacles wrapped around her leg. *They've caught me*, she thought. She heard her horse scream and then she screamed, too, louder and louder as the suction cups on the tentacles clamped down harder. She was stuck in their grasp, she was never going to break free . . .

"Lisa! Breakfast!"

She opened her eyes and saw her dad standing in the doorway wearing an apron. The air was full of the delicious smell of melted butter and fresh coffee.

Lisa sat up in bed. Even though she'd been asleep for over eight hours, her body still felt like she'd just run a marathon. She gingerly folded back the covers and looked at her legs. No tentacles. Of course there weren't. What was she thinking?

A few minutes later she was in the kitchen, but as soon as she sat down to join her dad at the table, he got up with an apologetic gesture.

She realized he was wearing his work clothes under his apron.

"I'm so sorry, sweetie, but I have to go in to work today. Boss's orders, I'm afraid. Apparently I need to get started on that Nox Nucleus project right away. We'll have to do our tour of the island another day. Soon, okay?"

What a surprise, Lisa thought to herself. *What was it he said again? Everything was going to be different on Jorvik? Yeah, right.*

"All right," she replied. "See you later."

"Make sure you do something fun," her dad said. "Have a look around."

She just nodded.

He was almost out the door when he turned around. "You're going over to Jorvik Stables today, right? It would be good for you to meet some friends your own age again. Maybe even be around some horses. I put some money on the counter for you, and a map of the island. But it's probably easier if you use your phone," he said with a chuckle. "Call me if you need anything. I'll be back around five and I'm making dinner. I was thinking lasagna. Your favorite."

Lasagna was not Lisa's favorite dish. Not anymore. Lasagna was *Isa's* favorite. But she was feeling too sleepy to argue.

Her dad lingered in the doorway, hesitating. He turned around again, like he wanted to tell her something. But then he turned to leave.

"See you tonight!" he called on his way out.

Lisa looked around the kitchen—the empty pizza box, the papers, the clock on the microwave that let her know it was later than she had thought. Through the small window above the sink, she could see a gnarled oak tree with limbs so heavy they were practically tapping on the glass. A small squirrel was making its way up the tree. She heard the sound of a car engine and guessed it was the neighbors across the meadow.

Her first morning in her new home. She wasn't quite sure how she had imagined it, but this was certainly not it. Everything felt stiff and hard to adjust to, like when you first put on a new pair of jeans.

In the end, she finally got up and ate the breakfast her dad had left out on the kitchen island. She spooned some jam on top of her pancakes and topped them off with the fresh blueberries her dad had left in a bowl.

She idly picked up the free paper sitting on the kitchen table. A gold-colored card fell out of the centerfold. A gust of wind from the open window made the card flutter gently in the air before it landed next to Lisa's feet. She picked it up and read the text:

ARE YOU STAR MATERIAL?
Welcome to The Jorvik Academy for the Performing Arts— where dreams come true and stars are born. We are currently accepting applications for the spring term. Visit our website for more information.

At the bottom of the ad, which was printed on thick, elegant paper, was a picture of the famous singer Cindy. Lisa had heard her music but had no idea that she was from Jorvik or that she had been a student at the performing arts school here.

In the picture, the beautiful singer was standing on stage holding a sparkling blue guitar. She looked like a warrior woman with her mouth open mid-song and one fist pumped in the air. Powerful. Determined. Undeniable.

What would it feel like to captivate an audience like that? Lisa wondered if someone so famous ever got nervous before she stepped out onto stage.

How do you know when your life is about to change forever? Do you feel it before it happens? Or only afterward? What was this singer's life like before she became so famous? Lisa's stomach turned.

She decided to check out the school's website. What did she have to lose?

Maybe this could be something for me, she thought. Something new. Something other than horse-related anxiety and a longing for a home that no longer existed because her mom no longer existed.

At her last school, she joined the school choir and took a guitar class.

Her teacher encouraged her to take private lessons, too, but she had never gotten around to setting that up, even though her dad had seemed to think it was a good idea.

When she found out they were moving to Jorvik, she wasn't sure what would happen with her music. Would the local school have good music teachers? Would they even offer music classes? She had no idea what to expect.

Lisa carried her teacup with her into what was going to become her dad's study. It was a good thing she had nagged him into getting the Wi-Fi up and running the night before.

She made a few Internet searches and discovered that The Jorvik Academy for the Performing Arts was actually one of the top music schools in the world. A few more clicks indicated that Jorvik seemed to be a hotspot on the international music map. How had she missed that?

She had been so busy dreading yet another move and her dad had been going on so much about the horses in Jorvik that she hadn't bothered to do any of her own research. For the first time she felt a tinge of excitement about this new place. Maybe there would be more to this island than she thought.

The morning sun had risen above the birch trees while Lisa filled out the school's application form. She wrote a long and passionate essay about singers and songwriters that have been important to her, her favorite songs, and her dreams for the future. She revealed things she'd never dared to tell anyone about, just contemplated in private. Meanwhile, she sang along to Cindy's most recent album and thought about how amazing it would be to go to the same school as her. Maybe they could even perform together one day?

Lisa let her daydreams sweep her away. Before long, she was the one on stage. Her acoustic guitar had been exchanged for an electric one.

Stars, stars, stars in your eyes, she sang, looking straight out into the faceless audience and the empty kitchen. She wrote the song herself last year but had never sung it to anyone.

The tea in the blue floral cup had gone cold. She walked back into the kitchen to make a fresh cup. While the tea was brewing, she checked the fridge and started making a grocery list. Milk, apple juice, cheese, Greek yogurt with honey, and fruit. She sighed. Could she just write "EVERYTHING" on the list and give to her dad, or did she need to be more specific?

In the end, she realized she was postponing the unavoidable. She *had* to go to the stables today and give the saddlebag back to Alex. She'd have to finish her application another day. She returned to the computer and saved the application for later. With butterflies in her stomach and last night's nightmare running through her body like a dull, thumping baseline, she put her shoes on, checked the map, and unlocked the front door.

The bike her dad had mentioned was parked in the driveway. It looked brand new, with well-pumped tires and fancy, complicated-looking gears. Lisa strapped Alex's saddlebag onto the panniers and then sat down on one of the porch steps. An old lady was walking her dog in the meadow. She waved cheerily to Lisa when she spotted her. Lisa waved back and opened Google Maps on her phone. She didn't want to bother with her dad's printed map—how old-school could you get?

The sun was warm. Lisa grabbed her water bottle and then locked the door behind her.

Okay, she told herself as she stepped back out onto the porch. *Now or never.*

She checked the map on her phone one last time to get her bearings, and then she was off. She pedaled just fast enough to keep the unpleasant thoughts at bay. For a while, at least.

The smell of warm pine needles filled her nose as she rode along the winding roads, trying to remember the way.

The road got narrower and narrower, becoming more of a path than a road. The surface was bumpy from all the hoof tracks in the mud. She stopped to check her phone again to make sure that she was on the right track.

It shouldn't be much farther now.

5

Finally—though it still really felt too soon—Lisa was standing outside the intricate wrought iron gates of Jorvik Stables, which were flanked on either side by two rearing, marble horses. From a distance, she could see a few riders in a meadow that began where the stable yard ended. Beyond that, there was a glimpse of forest and, farther still, high mountains against the blue horizon. Behind the stable was the sparkling blue of the sea. It looked like a painting.

The main stable seemed to be large and well kept, with several paddocks, indoor rings, and stable buildings. It was surrounded by a wall that had been constructed from the same pale-yellow bricks as the buildings. It was far bigger than Lisa's previous stable.

She parked her bike in the bike rack. There was someone saddling up in the gravel yard outside the main entrance. Lisa recognized her jacket. The girl turned around—it was Alex. She lit up when she spotted Lisa.

"Oh, hi, Lisa! You came!" Alex smiled, squinting in the bright sun. "It's so hot today; do you want something to drink?"

Alex patted her horse. Before Lisa had time to reply, Alex threw her the reins, "Here, would you hold him? I'll be right back."

Lisa felt like her legs were going to buckle. She was almost afraid to breathe.

But Tin-Can didn't seem to care at all that she was there as he suddenly moved over toward the lawn. He was calm but determined. Lisa wished she could be either of those things. She dropped the reins and felt the panic building inside her. What if he bolted?

Tin-Can stopped and gave Lisa a playful look. She went completely stiff when he suddenly began nuzzling her. She instinctively picked the reins back up and held them loosely in her hands. Her heart was thumping so loudly inside her chest that she thought everyone must be able to hear it: Tin-Can; the mother returning to her car after dropping off a group of excited kids; even Alex, who was now coming back out from the stable with two cans of soda.

Alex laughed when she spotted Tin-Can. "Don't mind him! He always does that. Here, I got us some drinks from the vending machine."

"Thanks! That's so nice of you." Lisa took a sip. "I think I got a bit lost on my way here. Oh, and I almost forgot . . ." She hesitated before handing the saddlebag over to Alex with a small smile. "Did you miss this?"

"Oh, thank you! I thought it must have fallen off in the woods somewhere. It's so nice of you to bring it over! You're staying for a bit, right?"

Lisa was about to say she unfortunately needed to go home, but Alex happily pressed on.

"Wait here while I get Herman. He's the owner of the stables. He can show you all the horses while I exercise this lunatic. Tin-Can goes nuts if he's not taken out every day."

Tin-Can snorted loudly and shook his head impatiently, almost head butting Alex when she leaned forward to adjust the bridle. Lisa could feel herself flinch involuntarily, but Alex just laughed and pulled a bruised apple out of her saddlebag to give to her horse.

Lisa forced herself to look at Tin-Can. He was actually really pretty, with an unruly forelock and mischievous air. Now that he was looking directly at her, his big brown eyes felt almost . . . human? If she didn't know any better, she would have thought he was trying to tell her something. That made Lisa feel really uncomfortable, so she looked away.

"Herman!" Alex hollered in the direction of the open stable door. "We have a guest!"

A middle-aged man with long, gray hair pulled back into a ponytail and thick sideburns poked his head out.

He gave them a big smile and came over to say hello. Lisa's thin hand was enveloped by one of his enormous gloves, marked by years of stable work. His handshake was firm.

"Nice to meet you! I'm Herman. I own this amazing place. Yep, the whole shebang! Welcome to Jorvik Stables! Sabine, was it?"

Lisa threw an inquiring glance in Alex's direction, but she had already mounted Tin-Can and was walking off toward the paddock. Lisa met Herman's kind, blue eyes.

"Uh . . . ?" she finally managed to blurt out. "Lisa. My name is Lisa."

"Aha. I see. I . . . " Herman seemed to consider explaining himself for just a second but then changed the subject instead. "You're new here in Jorvik, aren't you?"

"Yes, I arrived yesterday," she replied. A voice inside her screamed that she'd stayed far too long. It was time to go.

Time to go? another voice whispered inside her. *You only just got here!*

"Then let me show you the stables, Lisa. This is actually one of Jorvik's oldest stables and it has a proud history, let me tell you.

38

Once upon a time, Jorvik Stables used to be the royal stable. It peaked in size during Jon Jarl's reign in the thirteenth century, but it's been remodeled and modernized many times since, of course ..."

Herman continued to babble on while he led her into the stable, but Lisa had stopped listening. All these unfamiliar impressions had put her senses on high alert. Lisa tread carefully, as if she were walking on eggshells. However, the air was sweet with hay and the warmth emanating off the horses.

The smell seemed like it was speaking to her: *Relax. Come in.*

But her body was having none of this. Lisa had been thrown into those dark corners of her memory she preferred to avoid.

Mom, saddling her horse for the last time.

Mom's long, black hair in a thick plait bouncing as her horse lengthened its stride.

Mom, whose voice, filled with glittering laughter, calling out for Lisa to keep up: *Let's race to that hill!*

The stable began to sway. Lisa had to lean against a stall to keep from falling down. Then a horse nuzzled her hand. It was too much. Panic raced through every part of her body. She could feel one of her arms tingle as if it were starting to grow numb.

She had experienced a reaction like this before. She knew what she had to do. Sit down. Breathe. Tell herself it would pass, because it eventually *would*.

Except ...

Not now. Not here. Not *again*.

Where's the stop button when you need it?

"I'm sorry," Lisa mumbled. "I just realized I have somewhere to be. I can come back another time. It was great to meet you. Bye!"

A confused Herman watched her leave. As Lisa hurried over to her bike, her cheeks flaming red, she almost collided with a tall, broad-shouldered girl riding a muscular, jet-black horse. The rider reigned in her horse, who had none of Tin-Can's playfulness. She glared at Lisa and it felt like her horse was glaring, too.

"Watch where you're going! Khaan doesn't like strangers. Not one bit."

As if emphasizing what his rider had just said, Khaan whinnied. Thick scars covered his muscular body. His eyes looked like two dull pieces of charcoal. His rider turned him around and they broke into a canter as soon as they left the yard. Lisa sank into a squat next to her bike with her head between her knees. She could have sworn smoke was coming out of the horse's flared nostrils.

Just breathe. *Breathe.*

Just when she thought this day couldn't get any worse . . .

6

"Ow! Ouch!" Lisa tried her best to avoid the collision, but by the time she looked up and saw the other girl, it was too late. Books and papers flew everywhere, scattering all over the school hallway.

"Watch where you're going!"

"Sorry!" Lisa dove to the floor and started picking up the scattered papers.

Her whole body felt bruised, as though she had rammed into something steel-plated.

The other girl didn't walk off, but also didn't help Lisa gather her belongings. Lisa thought she recognized the voice that had just yelled at her. The sharp edge to it. When she got up, she could see the face of the girl she ran into—it was the same unpleasant girl from the stables yesterday. The rider of the demon horse. Of course.

How did this happen?

Lisa's morning had not exactly gone according to plan. She had played out a number of scenarios in her head about what her first day of school in Jorvik would be like. Oversleeping hadn't featured in any of them. And yet, that's exactly what happened. She must have forgotten to set her clock to Jorvik time.

She had woken with a start to the sound of a car engine. Tires against gravel, birds singing loudly. It was very bright outside. Too bright.

Lisa reached for her alarm clock, rubbed her eyes, and stared incredulously at the time. It was 7:20 a.m. She had to be at school in forty minutes. Why hadn't her dad woken her up before he left for work?

She jumped out of bed, dashed to the bathroom, and took the shortest shower of her life. No time for breakfast. Was she going to make it by eight?

And here she was now, in a strange corridor that felt much too long and dark, facing off with the most unpleasant girl in Jorvik. A small group of students had stopped to gawk on their way into a nearby classroom. One of them was Alex, who broke away from the group and walked up to Lisa.

"Hiya! Where did you sneak off to yesterday? Come on, I'll take you to the office so you can get your schedule. If we have chemistry together, you could be my lab partner. My previous one got, uh, tired of my experiments. She preferred the periodic table to action, if you catch my drift. But you look like you like chemistry, too— am I right or am I right?"

Before Lisa had a chance to answer, Alex firmly grabbed her arm and walked her over to the office. The principal was waiting to give her a welcome speech, locker keys, her schedule, and, almost certainly, a few words on the importance of being punctual, because that's how it had been at every school she'd previously attended.

Lisa breathed a sigh of relief. She seemed to have already made a friend on Jorvik . . . and, as she thought about the girl who she bumped into, possibly an enemy, as well.

Alex seemed to read her mind: "Hey, don't worry about Sabine. She's pretty new here, too, but doesn't exactly seem to be keeping a low profile. Proper weirdo, if you ask me. Same goes for her BFF Jessica; they act as it they owned the place, always stirring up trouble and picking fights."

Great, Lisa thought to herself. *Two of them to watch out for.* Sabine seemed like the last person in the world she'd want to end up in a fight with; the girl looked like she could punch through a brick wall.

Alex continued, "They're both bad news, but Sabine's worse. No point speculating about who's peed in her cornflakes this particular morning. Her horse is scary, too. His name's Khaan. Did you see him yesterday? Seriously creepy. Tried to bite Tin-Can the other week, but he'll live to regret that. No one messes with my little troll pony; he's cockier than he has a right to be."

Lisa laughed. She noticed that it was easy to laugh when she was with Alex. She followed Alex to their English classroom to begin her first day of school in Jorvik.

After her morning classes, which were mostly spent forgetting the names of everyone she met, Alex led Lisa over to a slightly younger boy wearing a Jarlaheim Mustangs baseball cap. During their journey over to the island, her dad had told her the Jarlaheim Mustangs were the local basketball team. A very popular team, apparently. The boy in the baseball cap was dribbling a basketball through the schoolyard.

"This is my little brother, James," Alex said.

"Hey," he grunted in a faltering teenage voice without dropping the ball. Lisa noticed that both siblings shared the same golden-brown eyes. And they both had that look she'd already caught several times in Alex's eyes. It was a glint that seemed to promise pranks and mischief. It was also the very same glint she'd seen in Tin-Can's eyes.

On their way to the school cafeteria, they passed a girl with long, black hair and holding an enormous stack of books in her arms. She looked very serious but lit up when she spotted Alex.

"Alex, would you mind opening my locker for me? I can't get it open and I need to get a book out of it."

"Of course," Alex replied, and winked at Lisa. "The ones you're already lugging around clearly aren't heavy enough. Obviously you'll need more books!"

They both jumped when Alex broke into the locker with a bang. Pleased, she folded up her pocketknife—which *definitely* wasn't allowed on school property—and slipped it back into her pocket.

"This is Linda, a future winner of the Nobel Prize," Alex said. "Linda, this is Lisa. She's new to Jorvik. She's the one I told you about last night at the stable."

Linda Chanda smiled and held out her hand. Somehow, she managed to balance her stack of books, now taller by two—a history book and a thick novel—while giving Lisa a surprisingly firm handshake.

"Welcome to Jorvik, Lisa! Why don't you come to the stables with us after school? Though come to think of it, I should actually get started on my English essay this afternoon . . ."

"As if you're getting anything other than an A on it, Linda," Alex said, nudging her.

Linda waved her hand dismissively and turned to Lisa.

"I hope you'll like it here. Do you live near the stables?"

"Not too far," Lisa replied. "What about you?"

"I live here in central Jarlaheim with my aunt," Linda replied. "And my cat, Misty."

"And she has her own separate entrance!" Alex interrupted. "Extremely useful for parties, among other things. Shouldn't we throw one soon, by the way?"

"In your dreams," Linda muttered. "My aunt would never let me . . . I swear, that woman has a sixth sense when it comes to parties. Don't you remember when we had that sleepover at your place last summer and she just *happened* to turn up with a freshly baked pie just as we were about to start watching a horror movie?"

They continued walking toward the cafeteria. Alex suggested they sit out at one of the tables on the school's large patio. While they were waiting in line to buy their lunches, they discussed the big upcoming harvest festival.

"You have to do the Light Ride with us, Lisa," Alex said, her eyes beaming. "It's a Jorvik tradition. Everyone takes their horses out for a night ride during the Aideen Festival. Lanterns, horses, and people dressed up in old-timey clothes. It's really fun!"

On their way out to the patio, they said hi to a girl Lisa hadn't seen before. She was tall, blond, and looked like she was in a hurry. She accidentally bumped Lisa's arm, causing most of her milk to slosh over her tray.

"I'm so sorry!" the girl exclaimed. Lisa could tell her apology was genuine. She nodded and smiled warmly at the other girl, who rushed on through the cafeteria.

"That was Anne von Blyssen," Alex said after they sat down at one of the tables. She made a bit of a face.

"She's kind of full of herself sometimes," Linda explained. "Though she is an amazing dressage rider. You'll see her and her horse, Concorde, at the stable later if you come with us."

"Our horses, Tin-Can and Meteor, actually seem to be best friends with Concorde," Linda said. "You *have* to come with us after school today!"

The stable. Lisa suddenly felt herself close up. Was she really ready? Last time, it had ended with her fleeing the scene. She didn't think she could endure another panic attack, especially if

Sabine and her monster horse showed up again. Maybe even Jessica, too. What if Jessica also had a monster horse? She wanted to ask the others but was apprehensive. Because if that was the case, then that alone would be a good enough reason to stay away from the stables. Despite her fears, there was something about these girls. Lisa liked being with them. It kind of felt like a new door had opened for her. Wouldn't it be silly of her to shut them out without finding out what they and their beloved stables were all about?

"Sure, maybe," Lisa said slowly. "I just find horses a bit scary."

She paused to take a bite of her sandwich. She chewed it thoroughly before looking up, because she could tell the other two were staring at her as though she were completely insane.

"You . . . don't like horses?" Alex and Linda asked in unison. "But why?"

"Seriously, Lisa, I'm not even sure it's legal to move to Jorvik if you don't like horses," Alex said. "It's, like, in our constitution, or whatever."

"No, I mean, I do like horses," Lisa stammered, and wished she had something else clever to say. Something kind of funny to gloss things over, so they could stop talking about this.

"I actually rode for years," she continued. "But I was, um, kicked by a pony in the stable when I was twelve, and I've kept my distance from horses ever since. It probably didn't help seeing Sabine's horse yesterday. I thought he was going to attack me."

"Poor you!" Linda exclaimed. "That must have been so scary for you. But look, Khaan probably isn't as bad as he seems. You know, those creepy scars and the scary, rolling black eyes, and . . ."

"Yeah, thanks, don't remind me!" Lisa jokingly raised her hands as if trying to fend Linda off.

Linda pressed on, "Come on, he can't be that bad. He's a horse, isn't he? If I were you, I'd worry more about Khaan's rider."

"So, he's from Jorvik Stables?"

"No. I think Khaan's boarded at some private stable down the road," Linda replied.

Suddenly Alex got up from the table and signaled for the others to follow her. She looked like she had spotted something. Lisa and Linda left their trays on the table and followed her from the shady patio out into the verdant schoolyard.

"Speak of the devil," Alex whispered, tiptoeing over to the bushes that separated the schoolyard from the parking lot. "Look who has a visitor."

They saw Sabine standing by a monstrous, dark blue and green SUV with the letters *DC* on the sides and back doors. Sabine's head only just reached above the door as she looked up at the driver.

"Wow, you could fit an elephant in there!" Alex whispered. "What do you think they're talking about?"

The girls could barely breathe. None of them said a word. It felt like they'd accidentally strayed too close to something dangerous. A silent understanding hung heavily between them.

The driver had rolled the tinted window down enough for them to see that it was a man. The distance made it difficult to guess his age. His face had sharp features that looked as if they'd been carved from stone, and his skin was almost sickly pale. He was wearing a dark suit with a white shirt and an old-fashioned, red bowtie. Was he some type of businessman? That's what he certainly looked like.

While the driver spoke softly to Sabine, his fingers moved over the steering wheel like long, gangling spider legs.

The girls were too far away to hear what Sabine and the man were saying. Linda silently pulled out her phone and snapped a picture. Alex gave her a thumbs-up.

Suddenly, Sabine looked up, straight at the bushes where they were hiding. She sniffed the air like a predator. For a split second, she no longer seemed like a teenager in a parking lot, but rather something ageless and menacing. A cloud blocked the sun. Lisa froze when she noticed that Sabine's eyes were black and expressionless. Just like Khaan's.

Lisa shuddered. Were the others seeing the same thing she was?

The SUV suddenly drove off at high speed, skidding out through the school gates. The enormous tires left smoking tracks on the pavement. Sabine hadn't moved. She was still staring straight in their direction. Could she see them all hiding in the bushes? She quickly slinked toward the bushes. Sabine made Lisa remember a very strong tiger she had seen in the zoo when she was little. Sabine was tall and powerful and prowled along the bushes just like an animal stalking its prey. Lisa recalled the tiger's triumphant look when he proudly displayed his lifeless prey.

They held their breath, preparing to run.

"She's coming this way!" Linda gasped.

Just then, the bell rang. A group of loud students walked past them and moved toward the school entrance. Sabine gave the shrubbery one last look, then turned toward the other students. Finally, she started walking back toward the school building.

Lisa, Linda, and Alex exchanged looks. Linda slipped her phone back into her pocket.

"Do you think she saw us?" Lisa whispered breathlessly. They huddled together, giggling nervously. What was going on?

7

When the bell rang after their final class, most of the students were in a hurry to get home. Everyone except Lisa, who lingered by the entrance to watch her new classmates rush out, toward lives, activities, and interests she knew nothing about.

She had nowhere to go other than home, and on her way there she thought about what to do about going to the stables. When she said goodbye to Linda and Alex after lunch, they exchanged phone numbers and agreed to get in touch later. She was grateful they didn't demand an answer about the stables right then and there.

As she slowly passed the bushes where she, Alex, and Linda had hidden during the lunch break, she thought about what they had witnessed in the parking lot. The strange way Sabine suddenly resembled a wild animal. Lisa thought back again to the menacing tiger from her childhood experience before shaking her head to clear the thoughts. It was probably just her imagination running away with her.

When she got home, she finished her application to The Jorvik Academy for the Performing Arts and clicked the "submit" button. It felt good to think about something other than the strange events of the day. She texted her dad to ask what time he'd be home and what they were going to have for dinner. It was a while before her phone dinged.

Hi Isa! Checking things out on the platform today. Might be a bit late. Around eight, at the latest. Will pick up burgers on the way home, okay? Love Dad.

Lisa sighed loudly and replied: *Okay. LISA.* No love at the end.

She made herself a couple of sandwiches and ate them standing up in the kitchen. After putting the butter and cheese back in the fridge, which was empty aside from some leftovers from the weekend, she ran her fingers over the kitchen counter. It was already dusty. She could see the imprints from her fingers on the shiny marble countertop.

A silent and suffocating feeling came over her. She needed a distraction.

She should check her schedule and try to catch up on biology, where she was apparently behind. But that was going to have to wait.

She finally decided to ride her bike over to the stables after all. She tried to calm her nerves by singing all the way there, an old country song. She figured it might work as an audition piece if she ended up being called in to the Academy.

This time, she had an easier time finding her way. As the tall gates loomed ahead of her, her stomach contracted into a cold, hard ball. She hesitated for a second and then took a deep breath before walking her bike through the stable yard.

Linda was in the aisle of one of the stables, grooming a slightly rotund, chestnut-colored horse with a shiny white mane. The horse was chewing on a hay bale that had slid down onto the floor. A saddle, bridle, and a saddlebag of the same distinctive model that Alex had were all lying on the stool next to them.

"Oh, hi, Lisa!" Linda called out happily and waved to her. "I'm so glad you decided to come! This is Meteor." Linda stroked the horse tenderly. "My best friend."

Meteor didn't notice her and continued to chew.

Lisa decided to move a little closer to Meteor. *Have courage,* she thought, gritting her teeth. One step at a time. Baby steps. Linda smiled encouragingly.

"Meteor is the world's cuddliest horse. Would you like to groom him? He loves being groomed. He'll even fall asleep standing up. If you want to put that old fear of yours behind you, you won't find a better horse to practice on."

Lisa hesitated, but Meteor really did look friendly, and he was so busy munching down on hay that he barely gave her a nod. Meteor looked a bit older than the other horses in the stable, with gray streaks in his tail and mane. Even so, he still seemed healthy and strong.

He's probably a good jumper, Lisa thought.

She took the brush and curry comb from Linda and started grooming Meteor with long, even strokes. Her muscles methodically remembered what to do before Lisa herself did.

"You've done this before," Linda said.

"I guess they say it's like riding a bike," Lisa replied. "But I never understood that expression—I'm terrible at riding my bike! But this feels like something I did yesterday. Even though it's been three, almost four . . ."

She stopped, wondering if she should tell Linda the truth about why she avoided horses. Lisa felt like a novice when it came to the whole friendship thing. She'd never had a close friend. She wanted to open up to Linda, but she didn't know how. But she'd seen enough movies and TV shows to get that this was one of those pivotal moments. An opportunity to actually tell someone who wanted to listen.

Lisa braced herself. She blurted it out quickly, before she could stop herself.

"It was . . . a riding accident. I was okay, but my mom wasn't. That's why I'm afraid," she whispered.

Her tears came pouring out. At first, Linda looked slightly uncomfortable, like she wasn't sure how to comfort Lisa. Then she put her arms around Lisa and simply told her, "I'm so sorry." As Lisa continued to cry, Meteor stood motionless next to them, as if he were guarding the girls. They could both feel his warmth, his reassuring smell. Linda didn't let go, and Lisa was surprised to realize she didn't want to either.

"Thank you," Lisa said eventually. For a while, Meteor's stubborn chewing was the only sound in the quiet stable. Then the silence was broken by a few riding students leading their ponies into the stable after a lesson.

Lisa bent down and picked some straw from her sneakers.

Her eyes were swollen. Her voice wavered as she desperately tried to switch the topic to anything else but her.

"I'll tell you what happened another time. And thank you for the equine therapy. He really is super sweet, your horse. Actually, is he yours?" she asked. "I'm not completely sure how that works here yet."

"Meteor's mine," Linda said. "My parents bought him for me when we moved here as a bribe so they could keep working all the time."

"I know how that goes," Lisa replied. "My dad operates in a different price range, though. Takeaway food and ice cream money and such. In a year or two, I'll probably have eaten a pony." She paused. "I mean, not literally."

They both laughed a little.

Linda studied her horse lovingly. "I was born in Pakistan and we moved here when I was just seven years old. Jorvik is so completely different. It's like a fairy-tale island. We really loved it here, my family and I, but then my mom and dad both got offered jobs in the UK. They obviously wanted me to come with them." Linda paused briefly. "But I liked my school. I had friends. And I had just met this one." She patted Meteor tenderly. "I just *couldn't* go with them. So, they arranged for me to stay here in Jorvik with my Aunt Amal."

They were both quiet for a bit.

"Hey Linda," Lisa said. "Meteor. What breed is he? I can't quite place him . . ."

"He's a Starbreed like Tin-Can. Here on Jorvik, they have every type of horse in the world and then some. Meteor is one of the *then somes*!" She laughed and stroked Meteor's side. "They're still trying to figure out their exact ancestry. Some hippologists believe that Starbreeds like Meteor and Tin-Can are distantly related to some rare ancient horses that originated on the island." She smiled conspiratorially. "Some people even say that the Starbreed horses have magical abilities."

Lisa just nodded to indicate she was listening, but what could she possibly say to that? She could only agree that both Meteor and Tin-Can looked unique. Their eyes, their vibrant color. *Then somes*, like Linda said.

Linda told her more about the horses, the stables, and how everything worked. Lisa discovered she liked listening to Linda's voice. She helped clean Meteor's bridle and bit and noticed how natural it felt. She remembered how much she used to like this part of riding. The everyday stable chores. Fixing things around the stables, cleaning the tack—she could still smell the beeswax—and picking out hooves. The little tasks that were more important than the big events outside the stable walls.

Yes. She had missed it.

They kept talking.

"Other than Meteor, it's mostly lesson horses here," she said. "Tin-Can belongs to Herman, but Alex has kind of become Tin-Can's owner. Alex stayed on here after coming for a summer camp when things were bad at her house. I guess Herman wanted to encourage her to keep riding."

"Sometimes I wish I'd had someone like Herman after the accident," Lisa admitted. "You know, someone to persuade me to carry on. But everyone just tiptoed around me, all scared."

"Scared?" Linda said. "Of what?"

"Death, I guess," Lisa replied. "Being around it. Some people seem to think it's contagious."

She noticed Linda's pitying glance. "Alex seems like a blast," Lisa added, quickly changing the subject.

"She really is," Linda replied. "Alex is one of my very best friends. She stays here at Jorvik Stables for the most part. She actually lives in one of the summer camp rooms up in the main house. Herman is so kind in the way he thinks of both riders and horses. He's always on the lookout for the perfect match, and he really found it with Alex and Tin-Can. Did you notice that they even look a little bit alike?"

Yes, Lisa knew exactly what she meant. Suddenly, they were interrupted by a loud snort.

"And here they are!" Linda shouted, and waved to Alex, who was leading Tin-Can toward them. Both were out of breath, and Tin-Can's thick coat, which made him resemble an Icelandic horse, was curly with perspiration.

"We could both use a shower!" Alex hollered and laughingly pretended to wring out her T-shirt. Then she took off her helmet.

"What about you two?" she continued. "What are you up to? Talking about the lovely Sabine again?"

"Shh! She might be lurking about here somewhere!" Linda said, glancing around the stable. "After all, sneaking up on people seems to be her specialty."

"When people aren't sneaking up on her," Alex responded.

All three of them were in agreement. There *was* something seriously fishy about Sabine.

Alex walked off with Tin-Can and Linda continued to take care of Meteor. Lisa decided to explore the stable at her own pace. Sunshine trickled in through the grimy windows. Hay dust swirled through the air. She slowly made her way down the aisle.

She heard a deep whinny from one of the stalls as she neared the end of the stable. A curious head popped out. At first, Lisa instinctively backed away, but something in the horse's eyes reassured her. His eyes were so mild. Blue like the ice of a glacier. He seemed to be studying her, as though he could see straight through her. Her fear evaporated when their eyes met. Suddenly, her breathing slowed. She felt warm and calm. That hideous feeling of gasping for air, of drowning inside herself, that she normally expected in such a moment didn't occur.

She gingerly walked up and stood close enough to touch the horse's extended neck. He was as white as snow, and his mane, which she first assumed to be gray, was actually a very special shade of blue.

She almost stopped breathing.

Lisa opened the stall door, stepped inside and closed it behind her. A ray of light shone through the half-open window, and her heart fluttered as she took in the entire horse. Big hooves, a blue-tinted muzzle. He was a large horse, majestic in the way he moved.

She couldn't believe it—this was the horse from her dreams. And his name was—she opened the door a little and leaned out to read the sign she missed when she entered—Starshine.

"Hi there, Starshine," she whispered.

She should have been afraid, but all she could feel was warmth and affection for the horse as he put his head close to her and snorted. Lisa gently touched his muzzle. It was silky smooth and warm.

The horse snorted again and stuck his warm, heavy head into the crook of her arm. She let out a giggle and thought to herself that he was behaving like a love-starved puppy, despite being so big, such a lot of *horse*.

An electric warmth rushed through her. It was like a buzzing electric current, but painless.

Lisa scratched Starshine behind the ears, and he closed his eyes in pleasure. She stroked his glistening coat while he whinnied softly. He nudged her with his head when she paused briefly.

Lisa smiled. Just like with the stable chores, she'd forgotten how good it felt just to be around horses. How everything else—stress, bad teachers, and classmates that ignored her—just fell away.

Had she forgotten it, or suppressed it?

Trembling slightly, she put her arm around the horse's warm neck and patted him. Starshine stepped in even closer and blew air into her face. He smelled of hay and warm stable and something else she couldn't quite put her finger on.

Suddenly, Lisa was talking to the horse in a voice she didn't recognize.

"Hiya handsome, how are you today?"

I sound like I'm in love, Lisa thought. *Completely out of it.* She had never been in love, not really, but judging from what she'd read and seen in movies, she could guess that it was something close to what she was feeling right now.

It was not infatuation. But it was certainly something. All she knew was that she wanted to stay with this feeling a little while longer. It was as if the rest of the world had been erased. All that remained was Lisa and Starshine and the inexplicable, electric warmth between them.

"Ah, there you are, Lisa!"

Lisa was startled as she turned around and realized Herman was standing outside Starshine's stall.

"I see you've found yourself a new friend," Herman said with delight. "He's big," he continued in a tender tone, "but when he meets someone he likes, he's a real love puppy, as you can tell."

Then Herman looked at her apologetically. But why?

"I'm so sorry, Lisa, but I have to get Starshine ready and take him to the paddock now," he said. "A nice young lady is waiting to take him for a test ride. She came by yesterday and spoke to me about riding here at Jorvik Stables. Her name's Sabine. Beautiful name. Maybe you know her from school?"

Lisa shuddered. "Um ... Sabine ... ?"

"Yes. Very nice, did I mention that? And polite. It's not often you meet such a polite young person these days."

Lisa felt like the ground was opening up beneath her. They couldn't possibly be talking about the same Sabine ...

"She was only interested in Starshine," Herman continued. "She was very clear about that. Starshine's not exactly a lesson pony, and I told her as much. But with the right rider, he can blossom. Sabine feels like a perfect match ..."

Sabine? Nice? Lisa thought. She could barely manage to suppress a snort of disapproval.

She was completely confused. It was almost as though Herman was under some kind of spell.

Herman tacked up Starshine and led him outside. Lisa followed them, feeling helpless.

Linda and Alex were standing outside and saw them exiting the stable. Lisa mouthed to them, "Come quickly. Sabine! *Come on.*" She hoped her friends would understand what she was trying to tell them.

Alex and Linda managed to pick up on the fact that something was wrong. They followed her and Herman away from the stable.

Sabine was waiting in the paddock. It really was her. Apparently she was everywhere on this island. Starshine, who was calm as a cucumber a minute ago, shied and whinnied shrilly as Sabine pushed past Lisa to stand next to him.

Starshine looked at Lisa with panic in his eyes, like he was pleading with her to help him.

Get it together, Lisa. That's not how horses work.

"There, there, Starshine," Sabine said. Her voice was harsh. "Sabine's here now. It's like you've been waiting for me, isn't it?"

Starshine reared up, whinnied loudly, and tried to wrench free from her and Herman. Herman fought to hold onto him. Lisa felt an uncontrollable terror and put her hands on Starshine to try to calm him. She had no idea what was happening, but she knew it wasn't good. It was so very far from good.

Suddenly, Lisa wished she'd had the courage to tell Linda and Alex what she'd seen in the school parking lot. Sabine's dull, charcoal eyes.

Lisa looked over at Herman. His eyes were dazed. Freezing cold whipped right through her. It was as though a darkness was trying to completely engulf her. Put her to sleep. She could almost feel the darkness enshrouding her like a dense, pitch-black fog.

"What's the matter with you, Starshine? Calm down! This nice young lady is just going to . . ." Herman's voice was monotonous, almost robotic.

Sabine smiled at Lisa, an empty, horrible smile that made her skin crawl. Sabine reached out for Starshine and murmured something. For a second, Lisa thought she was going to strike the horse.

Why doesn't Herman do something? How can he just stand there?

"Herman!" Lisa screamed, but Herman didn't react. "Herman! What is going on?"

That woke Herman up. All of a sudden, it was as though he was back to his old self.

"By the light of Aideen . . . Get away from him," Herman shouted. His voice was powerful as he glared at Sabine. "Get out of my stables and never show your face here again!"

Suddenly, the sun slipped behind a cloud and the temperature dropped even further. Starshine collapsed. The big, majestic horse was lying in the sand, limp as a ragdoll. Lisa and Herman leaned over him. Somewhere in the background, Lisa could hear Alex and Linda shouting. Out of the corner of her eye, she saw Sabine sneaking away.

"Starshine, are you all right?" Herman panted, falling to his knees next to the horse.

Lisa followed his lead, throwing herself on the ground next to the unconscious horse. Everything happened so fast, before her brain had time to register what was happening. Her body knew before she did. And even though she was terrified for Starshine, her hands were steady. She placed them on his clammy neck and lay down with her face next to his. They stayed like that for a minute, until Lisa felt the strange, vibrating warmth she had sensed in his stall moments before. It radiated. The birthmark on her cheek prickled and burned. A melody, at once both strange and familiar, flowed through her like a trickling brook. Without realizing it, she was humming the tune out loud.

She continued to sing. Louder now. Pressing her hands harder against Starshine's trembling body, she felt a flow building around her as though she were lying in a fast-flowing current. An energy rushed around her, and she felt like she could almost touch it. It shimmered blue, pink, and purple.

Herman looked at her but said nothing. Could he see it, too? Starshine blinked one eye. Then the spell was broken by Herman's voice. The flow dissipated.

"Phew, I was worried there for a second. I was about to call emergency services for both you and Starshine. But it seems like everything is all right now. That Sabine . . ." Herman sounded grim. He scratched his head and looked like he wanted to say something else. Herman studied Lisa intently and then nodded to himself and looked away.

Lisa didn't believe in witches or spells, but how else could she explain what just happened? What was it that Sabine did to Starshine, and what had she done herself? And why was Herman acting that way? Did Sabine really do something to him?

Her head was pounding, and she realized she was so tired she could barely get back up.

Eventually, though, she did. She brushed the dirt off her clothes. Then she saw him. Starshine, who just minutes ago was sprawled lifeless on the ground, was now standing steady and regally next to Herman, who was holding his reins again. Starshine's sharp, blue gaze cut right through Lisa. Everything was spinning. The world warped.

What was happening?

8

Over the next few days, time stretched out like rubber bands, snapping back whenever Lisa least expected it. Slow hours at home alone were punctuated by a flood of new impressions at school, where time seemed to speed up. And then there was Jorvik Stables. When she hung out with Starshine in his stall, everything felt peaceful. She felt at home. There had been no sign of Herman the past few days. One of the riding instructors told everyone he had gone on a short trip.

Eventually, Lisa had her new routine down. For the most part, anyway. She hung out with Linda and Alex both at school and at the stable. She still sang, but only when she was alone or with Starshine in his stall. At those times, she allowed herself to fantasize about what it would be like when she was accepted to The Jorvik Academy of Performing Arts. In her dreams, it was always *when*, not *if.*

At night, she cleared away her father's plate when he failed to come home for dinner yet again. He was always working. During the afternoons, in an effort to get away from the silence, the half-unpacked moving boxes, and the dust bunnies at home, she went to the stable alone.

It was getting harder to stay away. It felt as though an invisible force was pulling her back there, again and again. It was as if there was a melody that drew her in and she needed to hear it again. It felt like something important she needed to do.

She was still scared to think about riding, but Starshine calmed her fears and even made her feel brave.

That night, she dreamed about riding Starshine again. Unlike the other night, this dream ended happily. They were jumping a course together. Lisa's stomach flipped as they flew over the fences, but she wasn't afraid. Was he trying to tell her something?

However, she couldn't stop thinking about the afternoon at the stable when Starshine collapsed. Thankfully, he seemed to have completely recovered. Herman had called the vet, who came to examine Starshine and couldn't find anything wrong with him.

And Sabine . . . Sabine seemed to have vanished, too.

"No one's seen Sabine lately, right?" Lisa asked. She was sitting in the cafeteria with Alex and Linda. She looked around cautiously, as though Sabine might suddenly appear if she said her name too many times.

Everything related to Sabine made Lisa turn cold inside. She tried to push the thoughts away. They're not rational, she told herself.

Alex and Linda shook their heads in unison.

"No. Nice, isn't it, that she hasn't been around?" said Alex.

"Here's something weird," Linda said. "I was going through the binders in the stable office last night. I figured I might find something on Sabine, her parents' number or whatever. I don't know exactly what I would have done if I'd reached them. Maybe told them what happened at the stable. When Starshine collapsed, Sabine just left. How sick and twisted was that?!"

That was hardly the most twisted thing that happened in that pad-dock, Lisa thought to herself.

"So, what happened?" she asked.

"Well, it turns out the contact details she gave Herman were false. The address doesn't exist. And Sabine's phone number doesn't, either. And here's what's really creepy," Linda said, her eyes big and round. "I called the number, and it belongs to a cemetery."

Lisa could feel goose bumps spreading down her arms. She pulled her cardigan tighter around her.

The buzz of the cafeteria was deafening. Lisa had to lean across the table to hear what the others were saying. Over by the serving counter, someone dropped a glass, and the sound of it shattering echoed through the entire room, followed by sarcastic clapping and jeering. Lisa looked up from her pasta salad and realized it was Alex's younger brother, James, who had dropped the glass. He tried to seem nonchalant, like he didn't care. However, when Alex got up to help her brother, she quickly sat back down when he shooed her away, clearly embarrassed.

Alex started thinking about something that had happened after school some time ago. Something she hadn't figured out how to tell her friends about yet. She was out riding Tin-Can one day when she heard shouts and disturbed voices coming from the football field on the other side of the meadow. One of the voices belonged to her little brother, James, so Alex urged Tin-Can to canter over. When she reached the fields, she found her brother tied to one of the goal posts with jump ropes.

She looked around, and out of the corner of her eye, she saw a much bigger boy fleeing the scene. She recognized him from school.

Not exactly a nice guy. She made sure James was okay and then rode after the culprit. She didn't have a plan. She just knew she wasn't going to let the bully get away. Rage seared like a hot lump in the pit of her stomach when she caught up to him as he ran down the road.

"Hey!" she shouted after him.

He turned around at the sound of her voice. Alex stayed on Tin-Can and held her hand up in a gesture to stop him. The moment Alex raised her hand. She felt a burst of energy, there was a bright flash, and the guy staggered back as though he'd been pushed. For a second, a soft pink light flickered before Alex's eyes.

She walked Tin-Can up to the bully, bent down, and said intently, "You. Will. Not. Touch. My. Brother. Again."

He stumbled to get back on his feet while Alex and Tin-Can stared at him.

"You're crazy!" he hissed and darted away. His jeans had ripped at the crotch, and she caught a glimpse of his underwear.

"That's karma for you," she said and patted Tin-Can.

Since that day, he hadn't made any trouble for James or Alex. She had no idea exactly what happened that afternoon. But she remembered the feeling of wind in her hair, the sudden electric warmth that rushed through her body, and how that boy had reacted to her hand without her even touching him. How there had been lightning. That pink glow.

"Hello!"

Linda snapped her fingers in front of Alex's face. She blinked.

"Where did you go?" Linda asked with a smile.

"I could tell you," Alex replied, "but I'd have to kill you. Sorry."

They laughed. Alex, too, though she could still feel the warmth of the lightning that made the magical power more real from her memory of that day with her brother. Suddenly the light in the cafeteria even seemed to have a pink tinge to it, like a sunset.

"How was Starshine yesterday, by the way?" Linda asked, turning to Lisa.

Lisa speared two green olives onto her fork before answering.

"Same as always," she replied, popping the olives into her mouth. "Calm and cuddly."

"I wonder what Sabine did to scare him," Alex said.

Lisa hesitated. Should she tell them more about what she had experienced? She didn't yet know how open she should be. Maybe she was the only one who felt like something weird was about to happen. Would she be breaking some kind of unspoken rule if she said something? Would they laugh at her?

She looked down at her pasta salad. Maybe it was her imagination playing tricks on her.

But she still hadn't been able to get that song she sang for Starshine out of her head.

None of them wanted to think about Sabine anymore, so they changed the subject. They talked about the photo shoot taking place at school during the annual Jorvik Fashion Week and the upcoming Aideen Festival. They discussed the harvest festival and the trail rides and how they were all a little concerned about the amount of reading their history teacher had assigned. They should really skip the stables today to go straight home and study if they wanted to avoid a night of sleepless panic, but they all knew that, no matter how hard they tried, nothing would keep them away.

Starshine greeted Lisa with the same rumbling whinny as the day before. She walked over to his stall and petted him tenderly. When she turned around, Herman popped up like a jack-in-the-box.

"Hi, Lisa, so great to see you again!" Herman said. "This one's been waiting for you all day. Don't you think it's about time?" Herman looked at her encouragingly. "I mean, you've been spending a lot of time with Starshine, or so I hear! It's obvious you enjoy each other's company. Time to take the next step. Why don't you try riding him in the paddock since you're here anyway?"

Lisa felt welcomed by Herman's invitation to ride Starshine, but was still scared at the same time and didn't know how to respond. As much as she enjoyed spending time with this beautiful horse, she questioned whether she was ready to try riding again. Did she even remember how?

Herman could sense Lisa's apprehension but continued to smile and pressed on. "As I've told you before, Starshine is a *very* special horse. He doesn't do lessons. It would be good for him to have some exercise. And Sabine is clearly not an option anymore, as I'm sure you understand."

He scratched his head and then continued, "Sabine . . . what a strange episode that was. I woke up with a pounding headache the next day. And I'm still having a hard time working out exactly what happened in the paddock. All I have is these flashbacks that I've been trying to piece together, but they make no sense."

He then changed the subject.

"Anyway, you can borrow a helmet and vest. I think these will fit you."

He looked down at the cowboy boots Lisa was wearing.

"Those will do just fine."

Lisa accepted the helmet and the vest and swallowed nervously. She thought about the accident, the fear, the anxiety attacks, about how everything was still so new and fragile for her at the stables. What if she ruined it all by getting back on a horse too soon?

Mom.

Then Starshine stuck his head out of his stall and lovingly nuzzled his head against hers, and everything she was worrying about dissipated. She adjusted the vest and put the helmet on. It fit perfectly. It had been over three years since she last wore riding gear, but it felt so familiar. She pushed her red hair aside and felt her face flush.

Ready or not, here we go.

What would Mom and Dad say if they saw me now?

Slowly, as if almost in a trance, she tacked Starshine up. There was a playful look in his eyes that she hadn't seen before. She followed Herman and Starshine to the paddock. The entire time, she was aware of how her heart was actually *not* racing, and how she was *not* having trouble breathing. How the horrible images from the riding accident were *not* replaying in her head. She realized that her legs felt a bit shaky, but other than that, she was okay. Actually, more than okay. When she stood near the other horses, even the gentle, sweet-tempered Meteor, she had felt a degree of unease. But as long as she was beside Starshine, she felt no fear.

They walked toward the big outdoor paddock. The air was heavy with impending rain, but Lisa wasn't going to let a few raindrops scare her away. Not now, just as she was about to face and overcome her fears. Her legs felt like spaghetti. She glanced up at Starshine, who looked completely calm. Out of the corner of her eye, she could see that Herman was studying the horse, too. Watching and waiting, curiously. They left behind the tree-lined road and the yellow brick buildings and walked out through the north gate, which led to the big paddock. Herman asked if she needed help mounting Starshine, but Lisa shook her head.

"I think I remember how to do it," she replied, grabbing a nearby stool. She climbed on the stool and swung a leg easily over Starshine's back as he patiently awaited her command.

They walked on slowly. Herman moved the stool out of the way and leaned against the fence.

Here I am, Lisa thought to herself. *Back in the saddle. On horseback. Stiff as a board.*

After a few minutes, her legs stopped shaking. Starshine walked forward smoothly and gently, peering up at Lisa. Can horses smile? If so, Starshine just did. She smiled back and felt tears welling up in her eyes. Only this time, it was tears of joy along with pure, unadulterated pride. She did it! She was back in the saddle!

After a bit, Herman asked if she wanted to try trotting. Starshine trotted for a while until he finally broke into a smooth, flowing canter. They were flying, as though they were one body. Lisa felt the humid air against her cheeks. She was intensely aware of Starshine's movements underneath her. She sensed that she was grinning from ear to ear. Starshine let out a loud whinny, and Herman just laughed out loud.

"I've never seen him this happy! Not since he sprinted about in the meadows as a tiny colt! I knew you were meant for each other! Would you like to ride out for bit? There's a great trail just over there. I know you can do it. I can tell you're an experienced rider, Lisa."

Without replying, Lisa steered the cantering horse out of the paddock, past a smiling Herman, who raised his hand in salute.

They continued out onto the footpath, past the stable gates, to where the meadow began. They then went onto the trails that carried them ever farther from Jorvik Stables. The winding paths were flanked by mossy green hills, and Lisa could just about make out the glittering waves of the ocean beyond.

She could also see the smoke plumes from the oil platforms far out at sea. She wondered whether her father was on one of them right now.

The wind in Lisa's face was in sync with Starshine's steady breathing. Suddenly, in the middle of a leafy group of trees, a clearing carpeted with soft, tall grass opened up. The clearing was bathed in sunlight despite the rain. There was a large stone mono-lith near the tree line. Lisa was too distracted to notice the pink runes starting to glow on its surface as she and Starshine rode past.

Starshine snorted. All Lisa could hear was the muffled rhythm of hooves on the soft ground and the creaking of stirrup leather against the saddle. For a second, she forgot that Starshine had col-lapsed in front of her a few days earlier, and that this was her first time on a horse in years. Perhaps they should slow down.

Just as before, Starshine seemed to read her mind, because he slowed down without her having to move her hand on the reins as much as a millimeter. He then whinnied and jerked his head toward the woods.

"What's the matter, Starshine?" Lisa asked. "Do you want to show me something?"

A horse and rider were waiting for them in a stand of trees. *Please don't let it be Sabine*, Lisa thought to herself. Starshine's ears pricked, and he let out a clipped nicker, as though he knew who it was.

As they got closer, Lisa realized that it wasn't Sabine. The horse was a gray Andalusian, elegant and strong, with a thick mane and tail. The rider was a woman, and there was something strong and proud about the way she carried herself. She was wearing a hooded gray cloak over a green tunic embroidered with intricate knot patterns. Not exactly standard riding gear, Lisa thought to herself. She was sure that she had never seen this woman before, yet there was something familiar about her.

"Hi, are you lost?" Lisa asked as she approached. The woman chuckled.

"Not at all," the woman replied in an accent that sounded somewhat old-fashioned. "I just wanted to introduce myself to you. My name is Elizabeth. I saw you the day you and your father arrived. Now I can see how well you ride Starshine, and I'm glad for it. And so are many others. I won't keep you any longer, Lisa. It was good meeting you. Farewell."

How does she know my name? Lisa wondered. Then it occurred to her that all horse people on the island probably knew Herman. He'd probably mentioned her to this Elizabeth person. Mystery solved.

Elizabeth pulled on the reins and turned her horse around.

"See you soon," she replied and cantered off.

Lisa thought that was a strange thing for her to say, as she and Starshine rode on. They worked their way up a long, winding incline and soon left the trees behind. The mountains started where the pine trees ended. She could see the bluish peaks ahead now, looming over vast, golden fields.

Lisa hesitated for a minute. What if she got lost? She didn't relish the thought of roaming about in the woods if it started raining. She felt she should turn back, but Starshine showed no sign of wanting to turn back. Instead, he accelerated into a careening gallop that sent the pebbles around his hooves flying. *I'm going to fall off*, Lisa thought.

But Starshine was the one who fell. Lisa barely had time to process what happened. Starshine had crashed to the ground, and Lisa heard a nasty crunch that made her heart stop. She could feel him trying to get back up, but his leg buckled. She slid off him as quickly as she could while he desperately continued to try to put weight on his foreleg.

Instantly, before she even touched the ground, she knew.

His leg was broken. Starshine was beyond salvation. At her old stables, the poor horses who broke their legs were sent to the vet to be put to sleep. There wasn't much else to do. Her tears poured onto Starshine's injured leg. She looked into his glazed eyes. There was something there, though. Was he trying to tell her something? He trembled under her light touch as she brushed her fingers over the injured leg.

She wondered how far away Elizabeth and her horse might have gone by now. Perhaps they could help? She lingered over Starshine's leg. Everything was lost. What difference would three or five minutes make?

I've killed Starshine, Lisa thought to herself. The words sent shivers down her spine.

Were her dreams supposed to be a warning? Should her journey with Starshine have remained in her imagination? She should have listened to them.

She got her phone out to call for help. Then a glow began to fill the air. At first, Lisa figured it was from the screen of her phone, but then she noticed rays that seemed to be coming from near Starshine's leg. The strange glow slowly rose through the air in twisting tendrils. She noticed a blue circle on the ground where they were standing. Inside the circle was a star-shaped, sinuous pattern.

Then a blue and pink shimmering band vibrated in the air between Starshine and Lisa. Where was this pattern of light coming from? She blinked her eyes in confusion. Had she hit her head without noticing? Lisa dropped her phone. Now a strong light was shining from the palm of her hand. As she slowly moved her hand in front of her, the light followed, as if she were moving through molasses.

The music returned, this time with a different song. Lisa began singing an ancient-sounding, melodic tune that made her think of mystical faraway places. But how did she know the words? The song just seemed to naturally flow out of her.

The light danced in Starshine's eyes and the freckled birthmark on her cheek became searingly hot. She touched it with her hand and saw her face reflected in Starshine's glowing eyes. Suddenly, she realized what the shape of the birthmark reminded her of.

A star. With four points.

The music had grown stronger. And she could sense a magical light pulsing through her entire body. Beneath her hands, she could feel Starshine's leg aligning. There was crackling, trembling, and dancing underneath his skin.

It was a good thing she was sitting down, because otherwise she would have been knocked to the ground by Starshine. To her amazement, he rose to his feet in one swift movement. Lisa felt for his bone, the one that was just broken.

"There, there, Starshine," she said while she examined him. "There, there, beautiful Starshine, lovely boy."

She couldn't feel any fracture, and Starshine impatiently stomped his supposedly injured leg as if nothing had just happened. The leg *was* broken—Lisa had felt it herself. Now Starshine was pawing the ground with his head lowered. He glanced up at her from under his forelock. The magical, blue-tinged glow lingered in his fixed eyes for a moment.

Lisa slowly led Starshine back to the stable. They treaded carefully to make sure he didn't have another fall. Somehow, he seemed steadier on his feet, while she had to lean against Starshine several times to keep from stumbling. The world swayed and warped, like Lisa had just stepped off a dizzying roller coaster.

They reached the clearing with the runestones. The runes were pink. This time, Lisa noticed that the runes were actually glowing.

Weird.

When the first raindrops hit her, she became aware of a woman's soft voice speaking to her inside her head. At first, she turned around to see if Elizabeth had returned, but there was no one there. Just Starshine and Lisa.

This is your gift, Lisa, the voice told her. *To heal and care for the injured and sick. Use your gift well. I will see you soon.*

To heal and care for the injured and sick.

She didn't quite understand how yet, but she had healed Starshine and saved his life. Lisa stared at the glowing runes until the light faded and eventually flickered out.

The rain made her hair wet and limp, and she slipped a little as she led Starshine back to the stable.

In the stable, Linda and Alex were weighing out hay for the evening feeding. Lisa was sure they'd be able to tell by looking at her that something had happened, but the girls seemed oblivious. Alex was talking about pouring oats into Anne's riding boots and Linda was giggling.

Starshine seemed to look at the other horses with some kind of silent equine understanding. Tin-Can snickered in response and

Starshine looked pleased. *Well, beautiful, I guess you're not really like other horses, are you?* Lisa thought to herself and stroked Starshine.

She sensed an affinity in the horses' looks. *None of you are like other horses,* she corrected herself. For a fraction of a second, she was about to tell the other girls what happened in the woods. Then she changed her mind. She didn't want to risk scaring away her new friends or, even worse, letting Herman know just how close Starshine had come to being fatally injured. What if he wouldn't let her take care of him anymore? Besides, who would believe her when she could hardly believe it herself?

9

Three drizzly days later, it was time to prepare the stables for another night. Carts of hay and molasses were rolled out in the aisles. Riders and their horses returned from the paddock and the woods. Parents picked up their children. Boys and girls cycled home with their headlights and reflectors on. A few wet fall leaves blew in through the open stable doors.

It had been three days since Lisa rode Starshine, but she hadn't dared to get back on him. What if something else happened and he got hurt again?

Alex and Linda tried to persuade Lisa to join them for the Light Ride on the upcoming weekend. They went on about candied apples and bonfires. Their social studies teacher had told them in class that fall was Jorvik's natural season.

"We should ride to Goldenhills Valley sometime, too," Alex said. "We'll see it when we do the Light Ride. They say it's always fall there. How cool is that? Halloween parties all year round! Anyway, *of course* you're doing the Light Ride with us! Now that you've ridden Starshine, I'm sure Herman wouldn't mind you borrowing him."

"Yes, you have to, Lisa!" Linda chimed in with a big smile. "I remember my first Light Ride on Meteor. It was the year that we had snow in September. We almost froze to death, but it was amazing. I think the weather's going to be better this year, so what do you think, Lisa? I'm so incredibly impressed you got back in the saddle again! What with the accident and everything."

"The accident?" Alex said, looking puzzled. "What, that pony that kicked you?"

Lisa bit her lip and Linda looked like she wanted to sink through the stable floor.

"Oh, sorry, Lisa . . ." she said. "I thought Alex knew."

"Knew what?" Alex asked.

Lisa felt their eyes burning into her. She had to get out of there.

"I'll be right back," she said. "I just need to go to the bathroom."

She locked the bathroom door behind her, sat down on the toilet lid, and shut her eyes. After a while, someone gently tapped on the door.

"Lisa? Are you all right?" Linda's voice sounded worried.

"Coming!" Lisa responded, but she didn't get up. The pipes clanked, and she saw a big cave spider scuttling across the concrete wall.

She thought about the events in the woods the other day. After a few sleepless nights, she concluded that she wouldn't tell anyone about what happened to Starshine. She had spent hours in his stall, squeezing every millimeter of his leg, looking for something broken or sprained. Nothing. Lisa knew that she should talk to Herman. What would happen if it came out later that Starshine was injured during their ride and Lisa hadn't told anyone? What if she—which is to say her father—had to pay the stable damages? She pushed those thoughts to the corner of her brain where she stored her secrets. It was starting to get crowded up there.

She had tried to reconnect with the healing power she discovered that day with Starshine, but it was fleeting. It ran through her fingers like sand. The magic seemed to be there, but she couldn't quite figure out how to hold onto it.

It was past dinner time and she should have been getting home, but she couldn't bring herself to leave the stables. Not yet. Her dad was back out on the oil platform and would be working there all week, so she was home alone. She wasn't afraid of the dark, but the house felt empty. At night, she wandered from room to room like a restless spirit, turning the lamps on and off, checking that all the windows were closed, testing that the front door was locked.

Can you ever get used to loneliness?

Her dad called each night before he went to bed in the platform's staff quarters. The Nox Nucleus project entailed a lot of overtime, he said. He asked her about school and the stables. He seemed happy she had started riding again, but the last time he called, he sounded stressed. Far away. His mind was elsewhere.

She got up from the toilet, washed her hands, and quickly checked her reflection in the mirror before going back out to join Alex and Linda.

"There you are!" Linda said with a warm smile.

Lisa didn't feel so alone anymore. She reminded herself that she was among friends. It was an unfamiliar feeling indeed. She smiled back at the girls, took a deep breath and said:

"Of course, Starshine and I are doing the Light Ride!"

· ✦ ·

That night, Lisa had strange dreams. When she woke up the next morning, she couldn't remember what they were about. That same song was stuck in her head again. Did the song belong to the dream? She didn't just know the melody, now she knew the words to what she thought was the chorus. She vowed to figure out the chords on her guitar after school. It really was a pretty melody.

The time is now, she hummed as she got ready for school.

The time is now, she hummed as she locked the front door.

"The time is now," she mumbled without realizing it as she ambled across the schoolyard. A boy walked past, making a circling motion with his index finger against his temple.

Lisa didn't care. She walked toward the front steps where Alex and Linda were waiting for her.

10

Somewhere along Jorvik's west coast, a colossal oil platform was moored at an old wharf. Large freight ships used to be built there. Now, the facility was deserted.

The platform was made of steel that was painted green and blue. A maze of pipes and staircases wound around the pyramid-shaped main building like giant, copper-green snakes. A bridge, temporary but nevertheless sturdy, connected the oil platform to dry land. Thick steel wires held the enormous structure steady next to the pier.

The searchlights carved into the darkness like hunters looking for prey. Watching. Waiting.

At the very top were the big, illuminated letters, "DC."

This was Dark Core's headquarters.

The waves rolled in. There was a bright flash of light in the dark, churning water. And then the portal opened.

A tall, thin man stood on a ramp up high. A dark suit and red tie could be seen underneath his long, olive-green coat. His pointy chin and crooked nose made him resemble a bird of prey. He had many aliases over the past few centuries, but most recently he was called John Sands.

In front of him was a strange contraption that was almost as tall as a small house. A round, glowing disc of fire burned like the sun in the very middle of the machine. Humming and rumbling, the machine kept the strange energy field running.

The man stared straight into the machine's swirling colors, utterly engrossed. The light of the strange energy field revealed that his eyes were black and dull.

"He can stand still like that for hours," said one of the two girls who had just arrived, both wearing long black coats to ward off the rain and wind. Each girl held the reins of their own black horse. The horses pawed the ground and nervously tossed their heads. One of them whinnied loudly and rather persistently.

"What's the matter with you?" Jessica said and yanked the reins hard. The horse fell silent.

Sabine turned to her.

"I, for one, am glad HQ is moored for service. I hate having to go back and forth on those barges."

"Mm-hmm," Jessica agreed. "I wonder what he sees in there. . . . He says he can speak to Garnok directly through the portal. I wonder if that's really true?"

She snorted derisively. Sabine shifted uncomfortably as she put her index finger to her lips in a discouraging gesture.

Not here. Not now.

The man suddenly turned and studied his visitors with his stone-cold eyes. Then he slowly walked down the ramp, without taking his eyes off of them. The horses' ears first pricked up and they both straightened up taller, as if to salute him.

"Mr. Sands. You summoned us," Sabine said, meeting the man's gaze.

Mr. Sands gave her a tart smile. "My generals . . . my two generals. Soon, there will be three of you, and then a fourth to complete your number."

His voice was a bit raspy, but he could still be clearly understood.

"Unfortunately," he continued grimly, "the despicable Soul Riders have also come together. The portal has told me this. The fourth Soul Rider has arrived on the island. This very moment, they are gathering at Jorvik Stables."

Every time he mentioned the Soul Riders, his words sputtered out in disgust.

"Garnok's deliverance has never been closer! Nothing must go wrong now. Am I clear? Nothing!"

Mr. Sands leaned in to Sabine's and Jessica's faces. The rain was pouring down, but that didn't bother him. His skin was as ashen as a corpse.

"You must act now! Stop them! I want to see the souls of those miserable horses devoured in the eternal prison of Pandoria."

"I'm sorry it didn't go as planned last time," Sabine admitted. "That redhead ruined everything with Starshine."

For just a brief moment, she resembled the teenage girl she supposedly was. Then her facial features changed and the hardened mask returned.

"And whose fault was that?" Sands roared. "I don't condone failure. Neither do you—or so I thought. The horses are the foremost allies of the Soul Riders in their pathetic struggle against us. Without the horses, their powers cannot be awakened. You know this."

"Same instructions as last time, Mr. Sands?" Jessica asked.

Sands studied them with his ink-black eyes. At first, he almost appeared to be laughing. But when he spoke again, he did so in a thundering voice that set the horses tramping about nervously again.

"You are now free to strike as you see fit," he roared. "Strike against the horses. Strike against the Soul Riders."

Mr. Sands raised his thin arms in the air. His white fingers were like stiff claws, and he raised them as if he were going to rip the overcast sky above him to shreds. He chanted on.

"Nothing must stop us now. Our cause is too important! Garnok is the only thing that matters! Once he is freed, this world will be mine forever! And you will finally be able to reconnect with Garnok and return to your world, ridding yourselves of your half-life here!"

He suddenly broke off. His voice was quieter now and that razor-sharp rasp came back.

"I've also dispatched some people to help you see to the horses. Some brawn to aid your brains. Time is short and we need all the help we can get."

He started pacing to and fro. The horses and their owners watched him.

"Soon, very soon, the third general will be here. It won't be long before she joins us. And then things will happen quickly, I assure you."

Mr. Sands turned to the portal. With his hands behind his back, he stared into the portal's pulsing, fiery energy. Little sparks erupted now and then. Just as Jessica was about to speak, he turned back to them.

"That's all for now. No more failures. You have free rein to act as you see fit, and help is on the way."

A few minutes later, Mr. Sands was in the back seat of a car, crossing the bridge, heading away from the platform and the wharf.

"To Pine Hill Mansion," he snapped at the driver, who immediately sped up.

11

The next Saturday, the whole stable was giddy with anticipation. Boys and girls raced up and down the aisles with saddles, blankets, water bottles, and bulging saddlebags. Many were dressed in old-fashioned costumes. Lisa spotted several velvet cloaks and even a Jorvegian folk costume in the island's colors of green, blue, and white. One of the riding instructors was helping a younger girl fasten a harp-shaped brooch to her dress.

Lisa looked down at the jodhpurs Linda had lent her. No one had said anything to her about dressing up. But then she spotted Alex and Linda walking toward her in normal riding gear, with thick knit sweaters over their vests, and she shot them a relieved smile.

Alex tossed Lisa a heavy sweater.

"Here," she said. "Better dress warm. It'll be past midnight before we reach the camp. Herman and a few of the organizers are going on ahead to set up tents for the Light Riders, so that we can go straight to sleep once we get there, if we want to. And believe me, we will want to. Last year, I was completely beat afterward. I ended up staying home with an awful cold for almost two weeks."

"Sounds more like an extreme sport than a cozy ride," said Lisa, who still wasn't quite sure what the point of the Light Ride was. They were going to ride in Aideen's footsteps and seek the Flame of

Jor, the spark that, according to legend, brought life to the island. That much she knew. But where were they supposed to find it?

Alex laughed. "Served me right for riding out when I was already sick."

Anne led Concorde out of his stall.

"Who are you going to the Light Ride with, Anne?" Herman asked.

"No one. I'm going by myself," Anne replied quietly.

The other girls looked at each other, trying to gauge each other's feelings.

"Ride with us, Anne!" Linda suggested.

Anne turned in surprise to Linda and smiled warmly.

"Thank you. I'd love to. If it's okay?"

"Of course!" Lisa and Linda said in unison while Alex heaved a small sigh.

They set off as soon as the sun had begun to dip toward the tree line behind the stables. Lit torches lined the trail. Folk music could be heard coming from somewhere, and a crowd of onlookers had gathered to see the riders off. A small boy handed Lisa a bouquet of flowers. She accepted it and thanked him.

"That's Jorvik clover," Linda said. "If you give Starshine a couple with his evening meal when we take a break, then he won't get drowsy."

So much to learn, Lisa thought to herself. She put the clover flowers in her saddlebag.

The Light Ride covered many miles, so they mostly walked to conserve their horses' energy. They stayed close together so they could talk. In the distance, they spotted a vast vineyard and a beautiful, gray stone manor.

The farther they rode, the more it felt like they were traveling out of time, away from the modern world to a mystical place where anything was possible. They rode toward the western part of the Northern Mountain Range, just beyond the large Silverglade Manor. From the summit, there was a view of Everwind Fields and a glimpse of the lights from Silverglade Village beyond it. On clear nights, you could see the lights in the castle windows.

Baroness Silverglade usually made sure the lights were turned on for the Light Ride. The castle served as a kind of beacon for the riders traveling through the rural southwest corner of Jorvik.

"Look at that!" Alex hollered as she pointed down at the dazzling fall foliage of Goldenhills Valley that spread out below them.

"What's that black patch?" Lisa asked as she squinted at the red, orange, and yellow forest.

"It's Cauldron Swamp," Linda replied. "I'd recommend steering clear of it. They say it's full of will-o'-the-wisps, the ghostly lights that lead you astray from the path so you become lost forever."

Lisa turned around and looked at Anne, who was riding right behind her. Concorde's ears were pricked as he nimbly moved up the hill. Lisa didn't see why Alex thought Anne was conceited. She seemed timid and withdrawn, if anything, as though she were afraid of intruding. Lisa gave her an encouraging smile. Anne smiled back.

Several other Light Riders were nearby, but they mostly kept to their own little groups. Sometimes they were alone. Sometimes there were plenty of others forming a long line of riders. Some sang well-known traditional songs about Aideen and the long journey toward brighter times. Lisa soon started humming along. Several people took the opportunity to stop at the crest of a hill; their horses walked on a long rein and stopped to graze occasionally.

Maybe it was the singing, the lights, or the soft evening breeze, but Lisa began to feel like anything might be possible. She felt like Starshine and her friends' horses were somehow linked together by an invisible understanding that had existed for a long time. And now that bond was slowly being transferred to their riders. Lisa thought she could see their horses exchanging glances, as though they were talking to each other. Linda had mentioned that Tin-Can and Meteor were of the fabled Starbreed. Lisa wondered whether Starshine might be, as well, and possibly Concorde, too. Were all four horses Starbreeds?

Lisa started to think back to the morning when she and her dad had arrived on Jorvik. And the near-accident in the woods with Starshine. Everywhere, there were stars. *Stars, stars in your eyes.*

"Wow! You have a lovely voice, Lisa!" Linda exclaimed.

Lisa stared at her. Granted, there seemed to be a song playing over and over in her head, *stars, stars, stars.* But she was absolutely certain she hadn't been singing it out loud.

"It's been stuck in my head ever since I first got here," Lisa said.

It was time. She could feel it. It was time to finally start talking. She took a deep breath.

"You know the morning I came to Jorvik? There was this strange glow in the sky," Lisa said. "And the stars were so bright even though the sun was just beginning to rise. I saw something I've never seen before. It was like a giant star. It's kinda hard to explain. It was so bright I thought it might blind my dad, but he didn't even seem to notice it."

"Star?" Linda said. "The thing I saw that same morning was like a moon. A big crescent moon. I remember, because I couldn't sleep and had gone out to fetch the paper."

"I saw a lightning bolt that same morning," Alex said.

"And I saw a sun," someone piped up from behind them. They turned around. Anne was riding along not far away.

"Come and ride next to us," Linda said. Lisa and Alex made room so Anne could come up alongside with them.

"*Starshiner, ray of sun, all the world is yours to keep,*" Anne sang softly and chuckled when she noticed how the others were looking at her. "I'm sorry, I have a terrible voice. But my mom used to sing that song to me when I was little. I don't know what made me think of it."

"All right," Alex said. "The sun, the moon, stars, and a lightning bolt. So we all saw different star phenomena that same morning?"

"That is so crazy!" Anne exclaimed. "There has to be a natural explanation."

"What does Google say?" Alex asked.

Everyone turned to Linda, who giggled.

"I didn't realize that was my new nickname. But sure, I'll have a look."

She held her reins in one hand and walked in Western style while she got her phone out.

"Find anything interesting?" Lisa asked after a short pause.

"I'm drowning in astrology sites with ugly nineties webpages!" Linda groaned. "All the flashing banners are going to make my eyes bleed!"

The others giggled.

"I don't know. This might be something," Linda said and frowned. "I ended up on some sketchy forum for researchers at Jarlaheim University. Listen to this: 'The sun, the star, the moon, and the lightning bolt are ancient symbols often associated with the legend of the four Soul Riders (see separate article). During an excavation in the Northern Mountains, carvings showing four riders were found on the cave walls. Researchers also found symbols that a local historian at Jorvik University later identified as a sun, a star, a moon, and a lightning bolt. The symbols are thought to be the source of the Soul Riders' powers and strength. The Soul Riders appear as the central characters in both paintings and poetry from the eighteenth century onward.'"

"Soul Riders?" Lisa mused, letting the words roll off her lips. Then her stomach did a backflip.

Anne slowed down Concorde, who seemed to want to trot.

"I've lived on Jorvik my entire life," she said. "How come no one—at school, my parents, relatives—has ever mentioned any of this before?"

"Hmm," Linda said. "I *have* actually heard about those cave paintings."

"Of course you have," Alex broke in.

"Yes," Linda said, ignoring Alex. "I've seen a photograph. Wait, let me check. It was something about a star. I can't quite remember." She searched on her phone. "Right," she continued. "A shooting star striking the rocky island jutting out of the sea. And a woman on horseback suddenly appearing along the rocky cliffs of the island. Another cave painting is of a person standing on the cliffs holding their arms out toward the sea—in what is thought to be a welcoming gesture—toward a shooting star coming toward him or her. You know what's funny though? The cave paintings are said to be around twenty-five thousand years old."

"What's funny about that?" Anne wanted to know.

"Well, there were no people on Jorvik that long ago. The first people supposedly came to Jorvik across the ice from Greenland about eight thousand years ago . . ."

Lisa listened in silence to the long, incoherent conversation about some goddess called Aideen who had apparently spread light as Jorvik was awoken and how this Light Ride was a tribute to her.

The idea was that the riders followed her footsteps all the way to the site where Jorvik was created.

They were then supposed to find the light Aideen was said to have placed there, which legend claimed could spread life across the island. No one knew exactly where that place was, though.

Lisa wanted to get back to the symbols. Back to the Soul Riders. She urged Starshine on and rode up to Linda.

"Isn't it super weird that we all saw different symbols?" she said while walking next to Linda and Meteor. "What do you think it means?"

"I was wondering *exactly* the same thing," Linda said slowly. She kicked Meteor, who wanted to stop and graze in a ditch. "Greedy guts," she laughed at the horse and shook her head. Then she fixed her eyes on Lisa intently. She looked grave. "I think we should go to the library when we get back to find out more, okay?"

Lisa nodded, and they left legends and strange constellations behind to focus on the ride.

· ✦ · ✦ · ✦ ·

Dusk fell. Several Light Riders lit lanterns and hung them on long sticks. Some had brightly colored paper screens around their lanterns. They shimmered in the dark night.

As they continued on their journey, Alex told a ghost story about a headless rider who supposedly haunted the woods on clear nights like this one. He was trapped in purgatory, doomed to continue riding until he found his head. He was unable to ask anyone for help finding it, because how could he talk without out a head?

Suddenly they heard the sound of twigs breaking. Lisa let out a small shriek.

"See! There he is!" Alex shouted, and laughed.

"Cut it out," Linda said and waved to a group of Light Riders who came out of a stand of trees. "We're almost at the first campsite now."

They watered their horses and sat down around the campfire where people were roasting hot dogs, marshmallows, and apples. The lights from the red and orange lanterns warmly flickered in the night. Lisa felt warm inside. Legend or no legend, something about this ride was doing her good, she mused. She realized she was actually starting to feel at home here on Jorvik. She hadn't even thought about her mom once today, which was remarkable considering she had been riding all day.

Until now.

She tried to repress the dark thoughts that were apparently lurking near the surface after all. Tonight, she wanted to be in the light. Linda caught her eye across the campfire and smiled. Lisa smiled back.

Soon it was time to move on. One of the riding instructors told them that the last stretch before they reached the overnight campsite was traditionally ridden alone, though each rider had the option to decide for themselves.

"They say that's when you can feel Aideen's spirit within yourself," Alex said and rolled her eyes slightly. Everyone giggled except Lisa.

"Of course we're riding the last bit alone. Hardcore! Who's going first?" Alex asked.

"I will," Lisa said, surprising everyone, most of all herself. The warm, fuzzy feeling from the campfire was still lingering inside her. It made her feel brave.

Something was telling her she was supposed to go first. She just knew it.

"Great!" Alex said. "Then I'll go after you, then Linda, followed by Anne. You'll need a flashlight for the last stretch to find your way in the dark, so make sure you have yours and that it's working. Call out if you run into trouble."

Lisa turned around and looked at her friends.

"See you on the other side," she said, smiling weakly.

"Say hi to Aideen from us!" Alex called out. They laughed nervously and waved goodbye. Lisa lingered for a moment as she noticed how the flames of the campfire turned everything golden: their hair, their beige jodhpurs, the plastic cups they were holding. She returned the wave and urged Starshine on.

The path was narrower now, and the forest suddenly felt bigger and darker. More desolate. The wind moved through the trees, causing the leaves to rustle. Other than that, there was complete silence. *Most animals must already be asleep*, Lisa thought to herself, and urged Starshine on. She wanted to get there quickly.

She began to wonder if she was on the right track. Shouldn't there be some sign of the other Light Riders on the path? But everything was quiet. Now that she was alone on the trail, the ghost stories that Alex told earlier felt so much more real. She thought about her father, who was probably already fast asleep.

The silence was finally broken by a soft, gentle melody that slowly grew stronger. A woman's voice. Was someone singing in the forest? Starshine pricked up his ears and snickered softly. Lisa held up her flashlight and waved it about, this way and that.

She dismounted and led Starshine off the path. There were fireflies in the air, which guided her. They whirred and jumped in the velvety black night. Lisa bent down and touched the ground. Her fingers grazed soft, damp moss. There was a light up ahead.

More fireflies? No, this was something else. The light crackled and glowed like a campfire, but Lisa couldn't feel any warmth in the air. It was getting colder out now. She pulled her thick sweater around herself more tightly and pressed herself closer to Starshine, thankful for the heat that came from his big body. She led him on, deeper into the woods.

The song faded away but the light from the campfire continued to flicker. Standing on the other side of the fire was a woman dressed all in white, with long, dark hair. She smiled at Lisa.

"I'm so proud of you, sweetheart. Soon, you'll be leaving. You'll know when."

Lisa thought she just might stop breathing.

The woman was . . . her mother.

Lisa stumbled, but Starshine's heft supported her. Her legs trembled, and she felt as though her heart was about to explode in her chest. But she had to get to her mom. Her mom! She was talking to her!

Lisa ran as fast as she could, but she saw her mother fade away right before her very eyes. She wavered in the wind for a brief moment and disappeared, piece by piece.

First her long, black hair, which Lisa had loved to hide in when she was little, then her dark eyes.

Her nose, the one Lisa supposedly inherited.

Her chin. Her mouth. The dress she wore when she married Lisa's dad.

Her red shoes.

Another gust of wind blew through and then her mother was gone.

"Mom!" Lisa shouted.

She raced past the fire to the spot where her mom had been standing just a second ago. She wanted to say something. She had so much to say to her, but her mom was already gone. The light had taken on a darker hue. Now it was fiery red, like smoldering embers. Lisa stood motionless as she watched the fire die out. She held her hand out to the spot where the fire had just been burning seconds ago, and gasped.

The ground was cool.

Everything was quiet.

Starshine nuzzled Lisa's cold hand.

She led her horse back to the path on trembling legs and then resolutely rode on until she reached a big clearing. She held her flashlight up and saw tents, horses grazing—and Herman.

"Lisa! Finally! The others were worried when you weren't here."

"The others?" Lisa said as she looked around.

"You must have strayed off the trail. They beat you here. Go find your tent!" Herman said. "The others are already making themselves comfortable. Crawl inside and I'll take care of Starshine. You must be tired, right?"

Lisa felt like she has just woken up from a dream. Her legs were still shaking as she unzipped the tent door and crawled in.

"Did you see anything?" Linda and Alex asked at the same time. They were already in their sleeping bags.

Lisa hesitated. She didn't want to talk about what she'd seen in the woods. She was too tired, and she couldn't possibly find the words. How would she even describe what she had seen?

Everything. I saw everything. Light, life, death. Everything came to me and then it faded and disappeared just as quickly. I have no idea what to do now, but my dead mother seemed to somehow know?

"No," she replied when she saw that the others were looking at her curiously. "I didn't see anything interesting. Just a big owl."

"We didn't either," Linda and Alex said quickly. Had they responded too rapidly? Lisa wondered.

"You know there are will-o'-the-wisps in the woods, right?" Linda said after a brief pause. "At least according to the old stories. They hope to lure travelers into the woods so they get stuck in a swamp. But luckily, we're actually pretty far from the nearest swamp."

In her dark corner of the tent, Anne raised her head. The screen of her phone illuminated her pale face. "Could we save the swamp stories for another night, please?" she said and put her phone away.

Lisa crawled into her sleeping bag next to Linda.

"Are you sure you didn't see anything?" Linda whispered.

"Let's talk about it some other time," Lisa replied.

She closed her eyes and thought that would be as close to sleeping as she would get tonight.

However, the next time she opened her eyes, the sun had risen.

12

Everyone was tired as they rode homeward in the golden, morning light. Tired, but elated.

The feeling of being a part of something so much greater than themselves was difficult to put into words. And yet there it was, in the pensive silence, in the horses' leisurely walk, in the chill of the morning air. The legend felt more real now that they had ridden in Aideen's footsteps. Everyone who took part could feel it.

"Did anyone have cool dreams last night?" hollered Alex, who was bringing up the rear. "They say Aideen might visit you in a dream during the Light Ride if you're lucky. I for one remember nothing at all. Typical."

The others laughed.

"And I forgot to pack my dream journal! Isn't *that* typical?" Linda sighed as she tugged on the reins when Meteor stopped to eat grass next to the trail.

"I almost never remember my dreams," Anne said. The mysterious look on her face made Lisa wonder whether this was actually true or not.

Lisa and Starshine were leading the way. She couldn't recall dreaming about anything in particular either. But the impressions from the night before were still dancing inside her. The will-o'-the-wisps in the woods. Her mom. The embers.

They rode the last part of the way back to the stables in silence.

13

The group met up in the school library the following day. They were exhausted.

Linda arrived first, straight from PE with a banana in her hand. Alex then sauntered in with Lisa hard on her heels. The last to join was Anne, who gave a huge yawn.

"These should be mandatory for Light Riders," Alex muttered, opening an energy drink. Linda snatched it out of her hand and took several big gulps before she gave it back.

"We'll have to bring it up with the principal," she said before opening a beautifully illustrated book about the horses of Jorvik and their history. Together, they flipped through the pages and searched for other information on the library computer's Internet.

"Look, a Starbreed!" Lisa exclaimed, pointing to an imposing horse with a shimmering mane as blue as Starshine's. "Before I came to Jorvik, I thought horses like these only existed in the toy collections I had as a little girl," she said fondly.

"I know. It's so amazing," Anne chimed in.

Despite their weariness, all four of them were ready to learn more about the legends they had discovered the previous night. At the weekend's Light Ride, it was as if all the old stories were speaking directly to them. There was no shortage of reading on the subject.

"Aideen might have been the first rider on this island, but she was far from the last," Linda said. "They say she was the one who brought horses into the world and that true goodness was born with her and the horses."

"Yep," Alex chimed in. "I've been reading about pretty much the same stuff. There are lots of different legends and myths. They all start and end slightly differently, but the contents are more or less the same. Four girls and their four protectors—horses, I'm assuming—will, according to the legend Linda was talking about, help save the world and defeat evil, a.k.a.... Garnok."

Alex said the last word in an exaggerated horror film voice and bent her fingers into twisted talons.

"*I will drink your blood! I am Garnok!*" she hissed. Linda laughed, but Lisa felt something dark clawing its way into her. She looked away. Alex's smile stiffened and disappeared when she noticed.

"Oh, did I actually scare you? I'm sorry! Can you bear hearing a bit more about this bad guy, Garnok? I promise not to bring out the fake talons again."

"Thanks," Anne said, nudging Lisa. "Not everyone likes a horror film before lunch, you know."

Lisa smiled weakly. She was happy to have Anne on her side. She was not afraid of the dark, and not usually frightened by ghost stories, but the events of the past few weeks had changed her. She was no longer certain about what was real and what was not. She wasn't even sure whether the Soul Riders existed, and as for Aideen, who once brought light to Jorvik . . .

What was the saying? Where there's light, darkness must also exist and vice versa? If that was true, then was there possibly the chance that Garnok might be real, too?

Alex turned the pages of the book in front of her and said, "Some historians have interpreted the cave paintings to mean that

Garnok brought evil and darkness into the world. You know, the same way Aideen brought the light. They're not sure which came first, darkness or light."

"Is anyone ever?" Anne said quietly.

The others looked at her.

"What do you mean?" Linda asked.

"Never mind," Anne replied with a shrug. "Maybe just that things aren't as black and white as they seem in fairy tales. How are you supposed to know who is evil and who is good? But what do I know, I stopped believing in fairy tales around the same time I figured out that Santa Claus isn't real."

Lisa opened her mouth to reply but was too slow.

Alex checked her watch and jumped up.

"Look at the time! If we want to eat before our next class, we have to hurry!"

The girls quickly gathered up their things and raced toward the cafeteria. It was only when they were standing in line and starting to load up their plates that they realized someone was missing.

"Anne," Linda said with a frown. "She didn't come with us?"

The three girls looked around. No Anne.

Anne was still sitting in the library among the open books. Her eyes were glued to one of the illustrations in a horse book. It showed a tall horse, a shining dark gray with a roached mane and white blaze. The horse was flying over the familiar green meadows she and Concorde had ridden across so many times before.

Flying, not cantering. Because this horse had wings. And it was so identical-looking to Concorde that Anne had to catch her breath.

No, Anne thought to herself. *I don't believe in fairy tales.*

14

Lisa's time on the island was passing so fast that soon the leaves on the oak tree outside the kitchen window had turned bright yellow and orange.

It was the last week before the fall break, and she was getting ready to ride her bike home from the stables. She didn't actually have a specific schedule to keep while her dad was away working on the oil platform.

When the sun had set and the horses had been given their evening hay, Herman pulled Lisa aside and said he wanted to speak with her privately. He looked grave.

Lisa was overcome with fear. The feeling of being caught red-handed was overwhelming. Had Herman found out that she almost fatally injured Starshine? Who might have seen and told on her? Elizabeth, the strange woman she had met in the woods?

"Let's go up to my office," he said.

Lisa followed him. Her legs felt stiff, almost as if they wouldn't obey her. They headed through the small door by the tack room and climbed a set of stairs to Herman's office on the second floor. He closed the door.

The office was small but cozy. It smelled like old riding gear and coffee that had been left brewing a little too long. Herman turned on the kettle and got the tea out. Before he took a seat across from

Lisa, he paced to and fro for a while. He opened his mouth as if he was about to speak and then closed it again. Lisa shifted uncomfortably, barely daring to breathe. Had Herman found out what happened during the Light Ride? Did he know she had special powers? Was he never going to let her ride Starshine again? Had she committed some kind of crime?

She pictured herself being thrown out of Jorvik Stables headfirst. Bye, Linda. Bye, Alex. Bye, Starshine, and goodbye to any sense of belonging. Tons of horrifying scenarios played out in her imagination while Herman tried to find the right words.

Four hundred years ago, they burnt people like me at the stake, she thought. It would be so like her to discover that she had magical powers on an island that turned out to be crawling with witch hunters. Why could she never catch a break?

He took a deep breath.

"Look, I wanted to talk to you about Starshine. You haven't been here for very long, but it's impossible to ignore the fact that the two of you have a very special bond. To be honest, I've only seen something similar once or twice before. It's rare. Very rare."

He offered Lisa a cookie and got up to fetch a couple of tea mugs.

"I'm not wrong in thinking you want a cup of tea, am I?" he said.

Lisa shook her head.

"Jorvik is a bit different from other places," Herman continued. "Maybe you've noticed?"

A series of pictures flipped through Lisa's mind like movie clips.

The strange light in the sky when she first arrived on the island.

Elizabeth in the forest clearing.

Starshine's leg—broken, then whole again.

Sabine's predatorial movements in the school parking lot when she thought no one was watching.

Sabine standing in front of Starshine in the paddock.

The runestone. Lisa's birthmark. The dark pull from the deep forests.

Her dreams.

The feeling of someone watching over everyone and everything.

Her mom in the dark woods.

Yes, she knew what he was getting at.

"Take our horses, for instance," Herman said. "Our island is world-famous for them. Some believe horses first came into existence here on Jorvik—that here is their absolute origin. The horses are a big part of what's unique about Jorvik. We have breeds you won't find anywhere else in the world. The horses here at Jorvik Stables are no exception. You might go so far as to say the horses choose us, rather than the other way around. Just look at Starshine. He's one of the most special horses in the stable. Well, I obviously don't need to tell you that, do I? But I thought you might like to know some background on him."

Herman picked up a framed photograph from his dusty desk.

"Aww, is that him?" Lisa said, going googly-eyed when she realized the picture was of a younger, and considerably smaller, version of Starshine.

"It is indeed," Herman confirmed with a smile. "He was just a little colt when we found him all alone up in Pine Hill Forest, on the other side of the Northern Mountains. He was so tiny, poor thing. He probably wouldn't have survived out there for much longer. The forest is a vast and dangerous place for a colt. Believe it or not, there were people who actually wanted to harm him. I brought him back to the stables and, in time, he learned to trust me. To trust humans. When he was about three, I broke him in with the help of several other instructors, but we were never able to make him a good lesson horse. Not a lot of people managed to cling on for more than a few seconds—until you arrived. It's extraordinary. He has really blossomed with you, Lisa."

Lisa smiled.

"No, Starshine's not like other horses," Herman continued. "Maybe it has something to do with his ancestry. We do, as I mentioned, have a lot of unique breeds here on Jorvik. Some are called Starbreeds. There's only a handful of them on the whole island. And we have four here at Jorvik Stables!"

Lisa already knew who they were.

"Starshine, Tin-Can, Meteor, and Concorde?"

"Exactly right," Herman confirmed. "We believe Starshine is a Starbreed of ancient Jorvegian ancestry. He has traits that aren't typical for any recognized breed. A Starbreed is very picky when it comes to who rides it, just so you know."

Lisa thought about Starshine's blue mane and tail, his ice-blue eyes, and the hint of blue around his muzzle.

Herman met her eyes and smiled.

"I've talked you silly now, poor girl! But that actually wasn't why I asked you in here. I wanted to ask you to become Starshine's groom. If you accept, you can consider him yours, more or less. You can ride him whenever and wherever you want, in exchange for looking after him."

"I would love to!" Lisa burst out. She leaped out of her chair. She had been expecting the worst, but this was the best news she could have received! She could barely process what Herman was telling her.

She wanted to hug him, but they shook hands instead. It felt solemn, somehow. Herman poured them another cup of tea and insisted they eat a few more cookies to celebrate.

"I baked them myself," Herman said. "Vanilla shortbread, my grandmother's recipe. Pretty good batch, if I do say so myself."

They really *were* tasty, Lisa thought, and she was suddenly aware of how long ago lunch had been. Herman looked happy.

"Lovely. I was hoping it would go this way," he said. "I will call your parents and let them know."

Your parents. Two parents. Herman obviously didn't know.

"It's just me and my dad," she said. "But he's going to say yes. As soon as it was decided that we were moving to Jorvik, he began been trying to get me back into riding. But now he's completely caught up in his work out on the oil platform. Some super important project."

She paused briefly, looked out the window, and noted that night had fallen.

"This thing that happened a few years ago made me quit riding," she explained. "Starshine's the first horse I've been on since."

Herman tilted his head to the side and looked at her.

"This is a very big deal, Lisa!"

"Yes, I suppose it is," Lisa said with a crooked smile. "Everything just feels so *right* with Starshine. He makes me forget about everything."

"He has that effect on people," Herman agreed.

They finished the cookies while Herman entertained her with stories about when Starshine was a disobedient young stallion.

"And one time, I found him up in Carney's vineyard, munching on grapes! His whole face was purple! He looked so guilty, the little guy. As though he were perfectly aware he shouldn't have escaped."

Herman and Lisa were so absorbed in their conversation, they neither saw nor heard anything, but in the gloomy darkness of the stable yard, something was moving in the shadows . . .

If one of them had been out in the stable yard, and had been paying close attention, then maybe they would have seen the two figures moving in the shadows. Faces half hidden behind masks, dark baseball caps, and long coats with big hoods.

And maybe they would have heard the whispering, too. Would they have noticed that one of the shadows, the taller and bigger of the two, was holding a cell phone?

"Boss, it seems like there are still a few people around the stables. But everything's quiet at the moment. I suggest we strike now, before they lock up for the night."

Someone said something on the other end of the line.

Suddenly, a blond girl rode past on her horse, much too close. She didn't appear to see them hiding behind the horse trailer.

"Message received," the one with the phone said. "We are a go. Talk to you later, Mr. S."

The shadowy figure slipped the phone back into his pocket and started walking toward the stable door with long, determined strides.

15

Linda was sitting alone in the school library. It was dark outside—even the janitor had gone home for the day. Students weren't really supposed to stay after hours, but Linda was a regular in the library, and she knew the librarian well. She loved the library so much that she had been trusted with the alarm code so that she could visit whenever she wanted. She had been in there a long time and she was starting to feel it. She was tired—she felt it everywhere, deep inside her bones and marrow. She rubbed her eyes.

Something was gnawing at her. It was trying to seize her and drag her off to who knows where. It was hard to resist the instinct tonight that there was something important just beyond her reach that she should know.

She yawned and continued to flip through *Jorvik Anno 1920*, the thick, dusty book the librarian got out for her before she left. She was working on an essay which was supposed to have "a local angle," and Linda had decided to research the Jorvik Hippological Institute and its history. She thought it was a great way of combining her homework with pleasure—she could finish her essay while learning more about the various stables on the island.

It's not like I have somewhere else better to be, she thought to herself, trying to push away thoughts of all the families who would be sitting down for dinner together at this moment. She felt a loneliness in her heart as she thought about how they would be smiling at each other while plates and bowls were passed back and forth. Sadly, this was not a regular part of her daily life living with her aunt.

When her parents were each offered professorships at Oxford—*we can't pass up this opportunity, honey, you do understand that, don't you?*—the idea was for Linda to go with them. But she surprised everyone, perhaps herself most of all, and chose to remain on Jorvik. Something kept Linda here.

Meteor.

It was decided that she would live with her aunt. At first, it seemed like a major step, but the unfamiliar soon became commonplace. She already had her school here, and her friends at the stables. Meteor, of course. And her cat, Misty, too.

Linda remembered how pitiful Misty looked when she first saw her, with her one intact ear and matted fur. The tiny, roughed-up creature, no more than a kitten, had turned up in the alley outside her aunt's place one morning and refused to leave. It was still there the next morning, and the next morning after that.

She contacted a cat shelter in Jarlaheim but eventually decided to keep the tiny cat for herself. Since then, Misty had become her true companion. She was more than a pet. A soul mate, perhaps. Sometimes, it almost felt as though Misty could tell what she was thinking. She was reminded of *spiritus familiaris*, the term sometimes used to explain a strong bond between humans and animals. But when Linda pictured the cuddly little cat who purred like an engine when she scratched her chin, she knew that Misty was not her "familiar." After all, only witches had familiars.

When she thought back to when she was younger, when her parents were always absent or lost in books and articles even when they were sitting right in front of her, she couldn't help but think that things were maybe better now. Now she *knew* she was alone, aside from her friends who sometimes stayed over and her aunt who cooked dinner and planned cozy movie nights.

There was a kind of security in this. She knew what to expect and didn't have to feel her heart begin to race every time she was promised something, whether it was a movie, bowling, or a parent-teacher school event. *We'll be there! Of course we'll be there!*

She no longer had to fear the disappointment she'd feel when she had to stand there, waiting for her parents.

She adjusted her glasses and read on. It felt good to lose herself and focus on something else. The smell of old, damp paper hit her nostrils, and she thought, not for the first time, of the amazing ability books had of immortalizing knowledge.

The page she read was illustrated with a black and white photograph of a large, imposing horse surrounded by men wearing hats and coats. Linda removed her glasses so she could take a closer look. There was something familiar about one of the men in the picture. She had seen him before, a long time ago, in another picture. No, more recently? Her brain worked frantically. She picked up her phone and swiped through her pictures until she found it. The pictures she took when they were spying on Sabine in the parking lot were blurry, since they were taken from a distance, and the view was partially blocked. She held her phone up and snapped a picture of the illustration in the book.

Something clicked inside her when she put her phone down. Something fell into place, but *how* could it be right? And yet, there was no doubt about it in her mind. The man in the old photo was identical to the man who was inside the SUV when they spied on Sabine.

Everything was the same: the nose, forehead, hairline, chin. If it weren't for the fact that the pictures were taken over ninety years apart, Linda could have sworn it was the same man. Could it be a relative? There was far too many similarities for it to be a coincidence.

Linda had a strong feeling her discovery was crucially important. She texted the picture from the book to Lisa and Alex: *CHECK THIS OUT. We need to talk. Now. See you outside school in 30?*

16

Lisa didn't hear the ding of the incoming text message from Linda on her phone. Herman had just been explaining to her that you couldn't move a Jorvegian horse off the island. If you did, it was said that it would die of a broken heart, since it quite literally lived off of Jorvik's natural environment. For these particular horses, their environment was no less important than food, water, or air.

Lisa made a mental note to say goodnight to Starshine before she left. Her stomach churned with excitement when she thought about how she was now the official caregiver of that lovely, wonderful horse.

The silence was broken by a sudden loud crash that came from below, followed by a scraping sound. Perhaps it was someone accidentally tipping a wheelbarrow full of hay over? All the horses whinnied shrilly. The scraping noise grew louder. Lisa and Herman stared at each other, bewildered. They rushed out quickly, sending their teacups and cookie plate flying. They raced down the stairs, into the stable. The horses sounded panicked. Something had happened. What was going on? Whatever it was, it wasn't good.

Lisa's heart was beating fast. They burst through the door by the tack room to survey the scene. The stable door was wide open. Several horses were rearing and kicking the sides of their stalls. One stall was open. It was empty.

"Starshine!" Lisa screamed.

Herman moved toward the main door while Lisa stared into the empty stall.

"Stop! You won't get away with this," she heard Herman shout in the yard as an engine roared to life. Lisa ran out. "I know everyone on this island. Do you think you can just steal a horse and get away with it?" Herman bellowed.

Lisa caught just a glimpse of the rear lights of a trailer as it disappeared out through the iron gate at a dangerously high speed. The sound of the engine was drowned out by the banging of hooves kicking against the thick metal of the trailer.

"They took Starshine! No!" Lisa screamed at the top of her lungs. *Why?*

Alex came running from her room in the main house. "What's going on?"

"Someone took Starshine!" Herman gasped as he fumbled to find his car keys. "Come on!"

The girls ran after him and jumped in his car.

Herman struggled with the engine. The car was old and rusty, but it had transported him safely around the island for many years. They couldn't hear the SUV anymore, and the engine wouldn't start. Alex leaped out and opened the hood with a bang.

"The spark plugs. They've ripped out the spark plugs!" she shouted.

Herman cursed. Then he did what he should have done in the first place. He called the police.

Alex ran toward the stable. "Wait here," she said to Lisa, who had climbed out of the car, as well. Minutes later, Alex came back out with Tin-Can. They had to ride bareback. There was no time to tack up. "Get on behind me. Now!"

Alex held her hand out and helped Lisa get up.

"Girls, please be careful, okay?" shouted Herman as he called the police on his phone. "It's going to be all right!"

"Are you okay?" Alex asked Lisa.

Lisa nodded. It was scary being on a horse that wasn't Starshine, but she had no choice. Starshine needed her help!

Tin-Can was a strong horse and carried his two riders with ease. They galloped along the road, following the tracks left by the SUV and trailer containing Starshine. For a while, they thought they could make out the red glow from the trailer's rear lights, but then the night went ominously dark. They stopped and looked around to listen. Lisa was fighting back tears.

"We're never going to catch up to them," Alex said, rubbing her eyes. The air was filled with a sense of panic. "Herman's called the police. They have to be able to find Starshine."

Lisa mumbled in agreement. Alex touched her arm gently. Lisa could feel that Alex was trembling, too.

"What are we going to do, Lisa?" Alex whispered, her voice breaking. "He's gone."

Lisa wiped away the tears streaming down her cheeks. What *were* they going to do? She had no idea. All she knew was that they had to get Starshine back.

"I don't know," she replied. "But I do know they can't get away with this."

She felt something in her break and collapsed against Alex's back. They sat motionless on Tin-Can's back for a minute. Without the light from the kidnappers' SUV and trailer, the road was pitch-black.

"Maybe we should call Linda," Alex said at last. "She usually has good ideas."

She pulled her phone out of her pocket and realized her screen was blinking.

"Linda's texted me," Alex said, showing Lisa the message. "Look!"

They both flinched when the man with the predatorial face popped up on the screen. Set against the dark of the night, he looked paler than before. They both shuddered.

"*Him?* Again?" Lisa said. She could feel the chill of the evening creep under her skin.

"Linda's at school," Alex said. She hesitated before pressing on. "Maybe we should head over there?"

"But what about Starshine?" Lisa exclaimed.

Alex turned around and looked Lisa straight in the eyes.

"We're going to find him," she said resolutely.

17

Linda was shivering as she waited outside the school building for Alex and Lisa to arrive. The evening was damp, and she wished she had brought a scarf. Still, she preferred to be outside right now. Staring at that creepy picture in the library had quickly become unbearable. She had to get away and move around. The restlessness she felt inside was even stronger now, and adrenaline was pumping through her veins.

Breathe. Move. It'll pass soon. They're on their way.

Recently, Linda had known things she shouldn't have been able to know. She knew, for instance, that Lisa was coming to the island even before she had arrived. When they met in the hallway in school, she recognized her instantly, even though they'd never met. She couldn't explain it. The last time she had explained to her aunt that this type of thing had happened, her aunt didn't seem surprised and had called it a premonition, a gift from the gods. Linda herself had never believed in anything except for science. She shut her eyes, trying to focus herself mentally.

The images in her mind washed over her like an uncontrollable, freezing shower. Everything was bathed in a pink light. She saw Lisa, who looked devastated. And Starshine? She could feel that something horrible had happened to him, but what? The images grew blurry. Linda waivered for a second, but then snapped back into the present. Something had happened in that instant. Something important she couldn't quite grasp.

Something . . . was missing, maybe?

Yes. Something was missing and they needed to find it.

Jarlaheim's town center was spread out below the school, glittering in the dark. There were not a lot of people out and about tonight. The medieval city became a ghost town around this time, months after the summer tourists had departed. Not even dog owners were out on their evening walks.

She shuddered, thinking for a second that she could hear the sound of clattering hooves. She peered out at the street leading down the hill.

Nothing. She must have been imagining that noise.

A few minutes went by and Linda was still waiting. But now, there was no mistaking the sound of hooves against cobblestones growing louder. It was getting closer, too. Then, suddenly, Linda saw Alex and Lisa approach on Tin-Can.

"God, I'm so glad you made it here so quickly!"

She stopped herself and looked inquisitively at Tin-Can and his two riders. Alex and Lisa both looked distraught.

"Starshine's gone!" Lisa cried.

"Gone?" Linda managed to respond.

"Stolen!" Lisa and Alex both blurted out at the same time. Their voices were shrill as they tripped over their words. Linda had a difficult time trying to understand what they were saying. She managed to make out a few words—"police" and "Herman"—and then went cold. She was right. Something had been lost. Starshine.

"What? Who would *do* something like that? Are you all right, Lisa?"

Lisa and Alex dismounted.

"I'm . . . okay, I guess," Lisa managed to get out. But she could feel the lump in her throat growing bigger. Somehow she managed to push it back down. There was no time for tears. Besides, crying wouldn't help Starshine. "It's going to be all right. Starshine will come back. He has to!"

She suddenly realized she must have said that out loud.

"Of course it's going to be all right! No one can get away with kidnapping a horse on Jorvik!" Alex said, with moist eyes. "No one!"

"Seriously, this is so insane!" Linda exclaimed. "How is this even possible?"

"It was surreal," Lisa said. "Herman and I were in the office talking, when someone must have broken into the stable. If I hadn't been there, I wouldn't have believed it either. It's sick."

"Okay," Alex said. "What do we do now? Wait to hear from the police?"

"I guess so," Linda said doubtfully and looked at Lisa. "Are you sure you're okay, Lisa?"

"No," Lisa finally admitted. "But I'll have to get by, for now."

"I don't know what I'd do if it had been Tin-Can . . ." Alex said, and Lisa noticed her golden-brown eyes darken.

The girls hugged Lisa, slightly lessening the panic that felt like it was going to break her apart. An enormous weariness was left in its wake and she sank down onto the ground. Alex took her jacket off and spread it out on the ground.

"Always prepared," Alex said. She smiled, but the smile didn't reach her eyes.

Lisa raised her head.

"I almost forgot why we came here," she said in a shaky voice.

"You had something to show us, didn't you, Linda?" Alex added.

Linda nodded.

"When I was going through old pictures, working on research for my paper, I discovered something I think might be important. I took some pictures with my phone. I sent you one, obviously, but there are more. I couldn't believe what I saw. You'll see what I mean."

Linda held up her phone for the others to have a look and pulled up the pictures of the mysterious man. The others leaned in closer to get a better look in the darkness. Linda increased the brightness of the screen.

"He's all over the old photographs of this island," she continued. "Look, I'll show you. At first, I thought maybe he had to be a relative of the SUV man, but he's *too* identical. We're talking twins."

"A twin from the early twentieth century," Alex said.

The slideshow continued. The man's sharp features and strange black eyes kept popping up. There he was with a strange-looking bowl haircut at a charity ball in 1965, in the front row at an auction in Jarlaheim in the summer of 1937, and they glimpsed him behind a broad-brimmed hat in the crowd at a horse race in September of 1922. It was always the same face and, despite the disparate dates, he looked to be the same age in all the photographs. In one of the last ones, he was standing in front of the gates of a big manor, next to an old-fashioned car. He looked like he was wearing some kind of uniform. A cap was pulled halfway down over one of his eyes.

"That picture was taken outside Pine Hill Mansion," Linda said. "It looks like he's the chauffeur. I wonder who lived there back then? We should be able to find out."

Alex remembered Pine Hill Mansion was an abandoned old castle with a remarkably lush garden, kind of like the setting of an old horror film. They rode past it sometimes when they went for longer excursions. She shuddered.

Linda raised one eyebrow.

"Want to take it one step further? I took my photo search further back in time, as far back as I could go. The photo quality's not great, but I found something interesting."

With a few swipes, Linda took them back in time to the end of the nineteenth century. They had to lean in over the screen and squint to see.

The sepia-tone photograph was filled with people dressed in old-fashioned clothes. Lisa started thinking about the song that kept getting stuck in her head. Horses. Fields. Tools. Harvest time, a crowd, and long skirts. Was this song related to a celebration, maybe? A little girl was posing rigidly in a dark dress in front of Pine Hill Mansion. She looked shyly into the camera. Standing near the girl, under a big maple tree, was the man. The same man.

Alex and Lisa went silent. They stared at the photo and listened intently. Tin-Can snorting was the only sound. Alex dug around her pocket for a carrot.

"That man," Linda said. "He *was* the man in the SUV, right?"

"Yes!" Alex and Lisa replied in unison.

"Exactly," Linda said, finally glad to get confirmation of the notion that now felt even more certain than before. Even though it contradicted the laws of time and space. "Those eyes. And the crooked nose."

"What we need now is high-tech facial recognition software," Alex said.

Linda kept tapping away at her phone and suddenly let out a squeal.

"Bingo!" she shouted happily and showed them her screen. "There's a caption here on one of the more recent pictures," she explained. "John Sands. The guy's called John Sands."

John Sands. Where had Lisa heard that name before?

All three of them looked up with wide eyes as they heard the unmistakable sound of hooves approaching.

18

The giant tree branches—pine, spruce, and birch—cast shadows on the ground in the early evening pink light. A girl on her horse was walking along the forest trails near Jorvik Stables. It was Anne and her horse Concorde. Even now, on a dusty forest path far from the stables' dressage ring, where no one could see them, there was something decidedly graceful about the pair. Anne's back was absolutely straight and her posture flawless. Her horse was on the bit, his neck perfectly curved. Anne leaned forward and patted Concorde.

"Good boy," she whispered. "Want to have a little canter?"

Her horse immediately picked up the canter and they were off. The dust whirled around his silver hooves. Concorde let out a snort and sped up a bit. Anne smiled, feeling the wind in her long, blond hair, which she was wearing down under her helmet for once.

Her evening ride on Concorde was always the best part of the day. She almost never met anyone, and she enjoyed the soft twilight.

Anne had preferred to stay out at night since her little brother was born. He was a much later addition to the family, completely unexpected—at least for Anne. Sure, he's cute, but Anne hated being woken up by his bawling in the middle of the night. She also worried that her mom and dad would someday push him as hard as they'd pushed her. She didn't want him to be subjected to that.

Maybe it would be different for the youngest of the family. She hoped so.

She liked how quiet the evenings were, both at the stables and out on the forest trails. Anne had spent many years at Jorvik Stables, but the chatter still drove her up the wall. How can people make so much noise while saying so little?

You know you wish you were a part of it, a voice in her head taunted. That voice had grown stronger lately. Anne knew there was truth in it. Her family donated more money to the stables than anyone else, and their name was everywhere on plaques and signs, yet Anne might as well have been invisible there.

At least that's what it felt like until this year's Light Ride. Maybe it was different now. Maybe . . .

They're just jealous, angel. That's what her mom used to tell her when she was younger and came home crying because someone had poured oats into her new boots, or put a lizard in the locker where she kept her clothes. As far back as she could remember, she nodded along and agreed with her mom. Jealous was what they were. That must have been it.

However, recently, it felt warm when she rode with Linda, Alex, and Lisa. Safe. She stopped seeing herself from the outside—she didn't have to overanalyze every line or movement. Is that what it was like to have friends? Anne didn't know if she could dare to trust this new, warm feeling that swelled in her when she thought about the Light Ride.

She had been burnt before. Girls had followed her home from the stables, acting like they were her friends. Then, after they'd been around Concorde and seen Anne's house, she heard them whispering about her in the schoolyard. Is that all she was to her classmates—someone to gossip about? How could she determine when somebody was being real?

She sighed heavily and urged Concorde on, standing up in her stirrups and guiding him over a ditch. Her big horse jumped it effortlessly.

They headed along a lit bridle path that led deeper into the forest when they were suddenly blinded by bright headlights behind her. Anne stopped, feeling like a deer frozen in the sharp glare.

The headlights belonged to a large, dark SUV that was thundering toward her. It was close now. Too close. She urged Concorde on. The engine roared as the SUV accelerated.

She heard the sound of tree limbs snapping.

Anne inhaled sharply. Surely the SUV was not going to try to follow her into the trees?

But that's exactly what it did.

Anne screamed.

She looked around in panic, trying to find an escape route as Concorde whinnied wildly. He stopped dead.

"Come on!" Anne shouted. "We have to run!"

Concorde reared up and Anne clung to his neck to stay on.

The headlights shone like death rays in her eyes. Anne tried to shut it all out. The terror at the thought of being run over had left her numb. Even though her eyes were squeezed shut, the world felt bright. She saw a pink glow behind her eyelids. It was seeking her out, that light. It wanted something from her. She grabbed it quickly, letting the light take her away from the SUV.

She could hear the engine, closer than ever, and then, suddenly, she couldn't. All the sounds folded up and then unfolded again. The world stopped.

Anne could feel the emptiness as the SUV ran through her and Concorde—but she wasn't there. It was as though she was standing outside herself, looking on. Everything felt slow and far away.

When she opened her eyes, she was staring at the brake lights. The letters *DC* were painted on the back doors. The lights flashed briefly and then it disappeared down the gravel road. A pink glow glittered around her and Concorde. Particles drifted toward the ground like stardust. Underneath her, around Concorde's hooves, there was now a circle of blue light.

It was as bright as the headlights were just now, yet completely different. More pulsating than blinding. Then everything went still and dark once more.

Far away, she could hear the sound of tires on gravel fading away into the distance.

Anne suddenly felt incredibly tired. The exhaustion almost made her slide off her horse. Concorde also seemed to be struggling to keep his balance, whinnying weakly and turning around. She urged him on toward the road. She was surrounded by the forest, which was as mossy green and shadowy black as ever. The forest she loved.

Anne let the reins go slack against Concorde's neck as they turned toward Jarlaheim's coastline. Anne had no idea how long they'd been out. She should have been making her way back to the stable but couldn't bring herself to turn around. Something made her press on. She was far too weary to make a proper decision. They rode on toward the town, whose picturesque streets were deserted. Everyone was home, having dinner, watching TV in their sweatpants, doing homework, or fighting with siblings. Anne felt as lonely and empty as the cobbled streets. She longed for her family's car and driver, who were probably waiting by the stables now, waiting to take her home to her warm, soft bed.

Concorde started to speed up. His ears were pricked. Where were they going? Anne let her horse have free rein. She was still shaking. Concorde neighed and was greeted in turn by a deep whinny. Echoes? He carried onward. He was not used to the road's hard surface but was well shod and didn't seem to be bothered by the new terrain.

The school loomed up before her. This was where Concorde wanted to go? They still had a way to go, but there could be no doubting the neighing sounds she heard coming from another horse. Waiting at the top of the hill was one horse and three girls.

Lisa, Linda, and Alex.

She didn't feel like seeing them tonight.

She didn't feel like seeing anyone.

Anne suddenly wished she could turn around, but it was too late. They'd already seen her.

"Hi," Alex said. It sounded more like a question than a greeting.

Anne rode up to them and dismounted.

"Hi," she said. "We were out riding, Concorde and I. Apparently this is where he wanted to go."

"Are you okay, Anne?" Linda asked, looking slightly concerned. "You look really pale."

Anne shrugged in reply. "This evening . . . I honestly don't know what to say."

"Nor I," Lisa sighed.

Anne suddenly realized that Lisa had tears in her eyes.

"Oh, gosh, did something bad happen?"

"Starshine," Lisa managed. "He's gone."

"*Gone?*"

"I'll fill you in on the way to the stables," said Alex, who had mounted Tin-Can. She hesitated a little, looking at Anne. "That's where you're going, right? Wanna go together?"

Anne changed her mind. Perhaps some company might be nice after all.

"I'd love to," she said and mounted Concorde.

Lisa pulled out her phone, which was flashing with missed calls. Three from her dad about an hour ago. A voicemail and a text. She read it.

Tried to call but you didn't pick up. Miss you. Back home tomorrow night. Love Dad.

It was getting late, so Lisa and Linda walked home. Meanwhile Alex and Anne rode back to the stables. After a while, Tin-Can halted and let out a long whinny. Concorde pricked up his ears and looked attentively at Tin-Can.

"What's the matter, Tin-Can?" Alex said. "Do you miss Meteor and Starshine?"

She patted the horse gently, and then she and Anne made the final push toward the stables.

· ✦ ·

White walls surrounded the laboratory with the beeping machine where Starshine was cornered. He roused himself when he felt Tin-Can's call. He tried to get to his feet and let out a drawn-out whinny, but was pushed back down onto the floor by rough, gloved hands. A syringe pricked his throat. Darkness engulfed the closed room, and with it, the island.

· ✦ ·

Tin-Can continued to neigh drawn-out, shrill whinnies as they slowly headed toward the stables. They echoed down the quiet city streets.

19

The house was empty when Lisa unlocked the front door. This made sense, given that her dad wasn't coming back until tomorrow night.

She realized that she just wanted to sleep and wake up to a new day. A new day when Starshine *had* to come back. Her longing for Starshine was physically painful, almost as if she'd lost an arm. It hurt just as much.

Before brushing her teeth, Lisa called Herman, who told her the police were taking the kidnapping seriously. They were at the stables, conducting a thorough investigation. But they didn't have a lot to go on. No one got a good look at the perpetrators or the vehicle.

Strange, Lisa mused. How could a big SUV and trailer like that just vanish on such a small island?

There was a pile of unopened mail on the kitchen table, exactly where she'd left it yesterday afternoon. She flipped through the stack. It was filled with bills addressed to her dad, the local paper, a few advertisements, and a thick, cream-colored envelope with a handwritten address on it. It was for her dad, but something made Lisa open it anyway. A folded paper fell out of the envelope. Lisa picked it up from the floor and gasped. A logo consisting of two letters rose up like blocks of granite in the top left corner of the sheet.

DC.

Just looking at those two letters made it difficult to breathe. Lisa unfolded the paper and skimmed the text.

Position: *Machine Technician*

Project Section: *Nox Nucleus*

Project Leader: *John Sands*

Dark Core.

Lisa shuddered. This couldn't be possible.

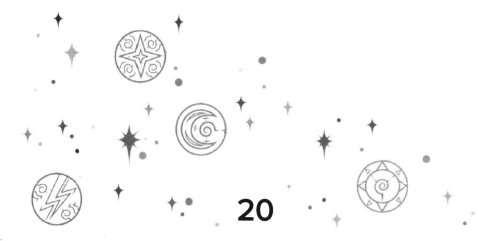

20

Carl was completely exhausted as he prepared to finally head home after a long shift on Dark Core's platform. The keys were already in his hand when he realized he didn't have his phone. Had he put it down in the lunch room up at headquarters?

Yes. That must have been it. He was in there during his break, trying to call his daughter, but she didn't pick up. Probably out riding. He must have left his phone there. The lunch room was several minutes' walk away. He sighed and turned back around.

The work to repair the platform in order to make it seaworthy meant that he hadn't been home for days. He had been informed that it was of utmost importance that the work wasn't delayed, but he had been gone too long. He should have been with Lisa tonight. Maybe even gone to watch her ride. His little girl, who had been terrified ever since the accident. The thought of seeing her mount up and take off made him smile inwardly, though. He should have been there.

The massive building was bathed in darkness. Only a handful of windows were lit.

He punched in the code to access the lunch room. His footsteps echoed around the big room. There, on one of the tables, was his phone.

He headed back out, thinking he was going to take the short-cut across the helipad when something caught his eye. What a strange machine, he thought to himself. Particularly that burning thing in the middle. It was like the eye of an enormous dragon. Or a cyclops.

He was well aware that regular employees were not permitted to enter the helipad, but going this way would save him several minutes and he wouldn't have to run up and down the steel staircases or cross the mesh bridges under the platform. It wouldn't be the first time he'd taken this route at night.

Just to be safe, he planned to keep to the shadows around the perimeter, even though the helipad appeared completely deserted.

He didn't know exactly why he was feeling so nervous. What did he think was going to happen? However, for some reason, he felt strangely like he was being watched. His mind traveled back to an osprey he once saw on a fishing trip. He recalled the way the bird soared above the mirror-smooth water in ever tighter circles until it suddenly plunged and snatched up its prey.

Was he the prey now? Whose prey?

A bolt of lightning flashed through the big machine, and Carl threw himself to the ground. He could hear voices now and pressed his eyes shut.

"Welcome, general!" The raspy voice belonged to Dark Core's eccentric and strikingly unpleasant CEO, John Sands. Carl stayed in the shadows, as though he were frozen in place. Could they see him? He was afraid to breathe. From his hiding place, he could hear a woman's voice.

"Thank you, chosen one," the woman replied. "I am finally free to do Garnok's bidding here on Jorvik."

"Which name have you assumed this time, general?"

"Call me Katja."

Carl could see two long shadows. He was just about to get up when he was blinded by the harsh light of a flashlight. And then they were on top of him. Two burly men grabbed him by the arms and dragged him toward the ramp where Sands was standing by the machine. Carl recognized them as two of the masked, strangely silent employees who had been lurking around up at the headquarters on the oil platform. As always, they were wearing long, dark overcoats and baseball caps under their big hoods. I must have missed seeing them in the dark, Carl thought, cursing his carelessness. Run, Carl, his gut had told him. Run before it's too late.

Now, it was too late.

Mr. Sands stared down at Carl as though he were looking at a speck of dirt.

"Well, well. Who do we have here?"

Next to Mr. Sands was a woman in white. Katja.

"You shouldn't have come here," Mr. Sands hissed. "You really shouldn't have come here."

The freezing cold air around Mr. Sands paralyzed Carl. It was so palpable he could barely breathe.

"Take him away!" Mr. Sands commanded. "Let him have a long think about what he's done. Long. Very long."

Everything went black.

21

When Linda arrived at school the next morning, Alex was leaning against the wall at the bottom of the front steps. She looked tired and Linda wasn't sure what to say about everything that had happened the night before. Alex seemed happy to see Linda and waved to her. Linda was just about to say something when they were surprised by the flash of a camera.

"Jorvik's Next Top Model is holding court over there," Alex said with a wry smile. She pointed up the flight of stone steps. On the top step, Anne was posing for a camera held by a good-looking guy with dark hair wearing a red sweater.

"I'm guessing Derek's eager to seize the opportunity for a photo shoot. Maybe even get a photograph in the paper now that it's fashion week and all," Linda said.

"Do we have time to stay and watch? By the way, where's Lisa?" Alex asked.

"I think she had an appointment with the principal," Linda replied. "I'm texting her now."

Linda's phone dinged immediately.

"She wants to meet up in the library later," Linda said. "Sounds important."

· +.✦.+ ·

At the top of the front steps, Anne put the finishing touches on her hair and then was ready. Her long arms and legs didn't know how to move until the camera flash washed over her. She smiled and hoped it reached her eyes.

"Amazing! Just like that! Just a bit longer! YES, delivering as always, Anne!"

For most students at the school, the photo shoot was an exotic and glamorous break from the everyday. But not for Anne. She had worked as a part-time model for several years and had been put through the paces by her mother in countless beauty pageants since the day she turned three. There was a special shelf in her room where countless trophies and diplomas jostled for space. Jorvik's Little Miss Sunshine, Little Miss Jorvik, Best Face, Most Talented, Most Beautiful Hair, Best in Show . . . Anne had them all. It was not always clear from the plaques whether they were awarded for her winning a beauty contest or for her horse winning a dressage competition. Anne thought that said a lot about how ridiculous it all was. Was there really such a big difference between her and Concorde? Between what was expected of them?

Prance about and win.

Ears forward, smile.

Repeat as needed for desired effect.

Yawn.

She would have preferred to throw away all of her prizes, but she knew how deeply that would hurt her mother. You had to be proud of your achievements. Achievements were like fuel in Anne's family. Anne couldn't remember a time when her life wasn't about keeping up a perfect appearance. She was never allowed to get dirty as a child. Her hair was always perfectly brushed; her clothes always looked freshly ironed. Sometimes, actually fairly often, she was jealous of the other children at the stables who were allowed to romp about in the hayloft, and get dirt under their fingernails and mud on their boots. Anne had been riding since she was seven, but she had yet to muck out her own horse's stall. It had become a running joke.

Anne yawned widely in front of the camera. *Mom wouldn't have liked that*, she mused, with a certain degree of satisfaction. She smoothed down her skirt, hoping Derek didn't notice. He didn't seem to have. The camera flashed away.

She wished she'd had a bigger breakfast.

She wished she were at the stables with her horse.

She wished it were warmer.

Never show weakness: another family motto.

"Thanks, Anne! Last few frames now! Jessica, you're up next!"

Anne suddenly heard her classmates, who had been watching the shoot, burst into laughter. She turned her eyes away from the camera and saw the new girl from her French class, Jessica, standing on the other side of the steps, making fun of her. Jessica craned her neck until she resembled a swan, fluttering her eyelashes and generally looking ridiculous.

Jessica fixed on her intently. For a moment, her eyes looked like deep, black holes.

"Look at me! I'm the prettiest and most important person in the whole world!" Jessica mocked, throwing the audience a kiss. "I'm Anne von Blyssen, such a noble name," she said with a lisp. Everyone laughed. This caused Anne to lose her focus and she stumbled to the ground in her high heels.

Her sheer tights ripped and she scraped her knee. Derek put his camera down and ran over.

"Are you okay, Anne? Are you hurt?"

Anne blinked back her tears and nodded through her gritted teeth. Where did they come from?

"Do you have what you need?" she asked.

"And then some," Derek replied. "Great job, as always! Time for school now, right? I'll see you soon. You're still on for the shoot at Jorvik Stables this afternoon, I hope?"

Anne hesitated for a second. Then she noticed how happy Derek seemed. She didn't want to ruin it for him.

"Of course," she said. "See you there!"

Anne moved aside. Before she could take a step further, Jessica swooped in and started smiling ingratiatingly for the camera.

Linda and Alex were waiting for Lisa in the library. They were trying to study, but it was hard to focus. How were they supposed to think about schoolwork when Starshine was missing? It was impossible to think of anything else.

"I had a thought last night in bed," Linda said. "What if Sabine knows something about the kidnapping? She did try to harm Starshine before." She fiddled with her thick braid. "I wouldn't be surprised in the slightest if Sabine was somehow involved."

"It's not like everyone on the island is suddenly wishing Starshine harm," Alex agreed.

"Exactly!" Linda picked up her phone and returned to the photo of Mr. Sands in the SUV, talking to Sabine. "They're up to something, those two . . . But what? I don't get it."

Lisa burst into the library, panting and brandishing a piece of paper.

"Your new schedule?" Linda asked, raising her eyebrows.

"Nope . . . Something much more interesting!" Lisa exclaimed. "A clue that might lead us to Starshine!"

Lisa placed her dad's paystub on the table in front of them and sat down.

"DC. Dark Core," she said. "Didn't it say DC on the SUV Mr. Sands was in when he was talking to Sabine?"

"Wow, Lisa!" Alex and Linda exclaimed in unison and gave each other a high-five. "This is it!" Then they broke off and looked at Lisa as though they'd been caught doing something bad.

"I mean, it totally sucks that your dad works for that company," Alex added quickly. "But good for our investigation."

"So, is that what we're doing now? Investigating?" Lisa asked.

Her stomach sank when she thought about her dad working for such a creep. Her lovely dad, who always thought so highly of everyone.

"Are you finding anything on Dark Core, Linda?" she said in an attempt to shake the thoughts about her dad.

Linda frowned.

"I think so," she replied and kept reading. Then she looked up from her phone.

"It looks like it's a really big company," she said. "It deals with oil, minerals, iron ore. Where there's natural resources, there's Dark Core. No environmentalism here. Dark Core's been around for ages, but I'm having trouble finding any concrete info. Someone's put a lot of effort into covering their tracks."

"And Sands is the head of it?" Alex asked.

Linda nodded.

"Yep, it says right here on this website I just found: the CEO of Dark Core is John Sands. Otherwise known as the creepy guy who doesn't seem to age."

A shadow fell across the table. They looked up and saw that it was Anne.

"Hi!" Lisa said and pulled up a chair for Anne. "Have a seat. We're talking about all the weird things that have been happening at the stables."

Anne sat down next to Lisa and smiled faintly. Her eyes slid over to Linda's phone. Lisa noticed Anne's face drop.

"What's the matter?" Lisa asked.

"I-I . . ." Anne stammered. Lisa held up her phone, so she could see the screen better.

"That SUV," Anne finally managed. Her face was ashen. "It tried to run Concorde and me over yesterday. Right before we met outside school last night."

Alex leaned in eagerly.

"Oh my gosh, is that true? That sounds insane!"

"Well, it said DC on it. Yes, I'm sure it was an SUV just like that one."

"Wow," Linda and Lisa exclaimed in unison.

"Nuts," Alex said and shook her head.

"I have to go," Anne said suddenly. "Concorde and I have another photo shoot at the stables this afternoon." She got up. "Maybe we can talk more then?" Anne suggested on her way out.

"Seriously, I don't get how she puts up with having her picture taken all the time," said Alex. Everyone knew that Alex hated having her picture taken—she even used Tin-Can as her profile picture on social media.

"So, we can assume Dark Core's behind the kidnapping," Lisa said. Her voice trembled. Could it really be true? Her dad's employer, a kidnapper? She continued: "It must have been the same SUV and trailer containing Starshine that went after Anne. The timing checks out, right?"

"Yeah," Alex replied in a strangely empty voice. That impish spark in her eyes was gone. "But I still don't get it. Are they trying to scare us? Threaten us? Or are they really after Starshine?"

Lisa pictured Starshine's shimmering blue mane and tail. His wise eyes that seemed to see right through her. It was painful just to think about him.

She was just about to say something when the bell rang. They had agreed to meet at the stables that afternoon, to watch Anne's shoot and tell Herman what they had learned so he could relay the information to the police.

"I'll have to join you later," Alex said, making a face. "Detention."

Linda grinned and shook her head.

On her way to class, Lisa texted Herman to say they believed Dark Core was involved in Starshine's kidnapping. She told him to let the police know. *Important*, she added in the text. Herman replied immediately with a thumbs-up.

Lisa checked her watch. Two minutes until her next class. She shot off a quick text to her dad: *You all right?* Normally, he always replied instantly, but now the seconds ticked past, and eventually her screen turned black as the phone went to sleep. She put it in her bag, figuring he'd certainly reply later.

The others rushed off to their classes, but Alex lingered in the hallway, absentmindedly toying with the lightning bolt pendant on her necklace. She always wore it around her neck, even at night and in the shower. She felt naked without it. But now, the pendant was suddenly scorching hot.

"Ow!" she exclaimed, rubbing her throat. She took the necklace off and slipped it into her pocket. She felt the heat from the lightning bolt through the fabric of her pants pocket.

22

As the last bell of the day rang, Alex gathered her books and started heading over to detention. When she arrived, the principal was making an unusual guest appearance to talk to her about how seriously she took the destruction of other people's property. Alex thought the prank she came up with—making the exhaust pipe on her math teacher's car whistle—was pretty funny. It wasn't like she *destroyed* anything. Not permanently, at least. She had just put a piece of metal in the pipe so that it made a funny noise when the car moved. Naturally, she refrained from saying any of that out loud. When the principal had finished scolding her, her eyes softened, and she said:

"You're a gifted student, Alex. That's why it pains me to see you in here so often. I know things at home haven't been easy for you these past few years."

These past few years? Alex thought sarcastically. *Try this past life.* She sighed, which the principal chose to interpret as agreement, and focused on the nineteenth-century ethics paper she needed to spend her afternoon on. As she wrote, she cursed herself for ending up here. She needed to be at the stables with the others. This was her last time in detention, she promised herself. Never again.

Progress was slow. The cursor in Word blinked at her mockingly. The minute hand on the big clock behind the teacher's desk moved at a snail's pace.

She pulled her necklace out of her pocket. The metal had now cooled, but there was still a burn mark on her neck and blisters on her thumb and forefinger. She spotted a small hole in the pocket of her jeans where the necklace had been stashed. *It is often said that ethics is about following your internal compass,* she wrote. *Some claim that compass is calibrated in childhood, when parents and other adults show the child what good behavior is. But what happens when the compass is skewed? What if we have been focusing on the wrong things all along?*

Linda and Lisa agreed to meet in the club room at Jorvik Stables. The first lesson of the day was still in progress, so they were all alone. Lisa made tea in the tiny kitchenette while Linda tried to coax some cookies out of the vending machine.

"Seriously, Herman *has* to fix this soon!" she groaned, poking at the flap. Eventually, a small package of chocolate cookies fell down. She smiled with relief and sat down.

"Linda," Lisa said after joining her at the table, "I looked up the name of that project my dad's working on. Nox Nucleus."

"Mm . . ." Linda immediately pulled out her phone and started googling. Lisa continued.

"Yes. Nox Nucleus. It seems to be Latin, meaning something like 'the essence of darkness' . . ."

"Or, perhaps, 'the Heart of Darkness,'" Linda suggested. "This is interesting. Did you know the Romans pillaged Jorvik after the end of the Bronze Age?"

"Is this really the time to talk about ancient Rome?" Lisa asked. Her head was already spinning with new information. Linda ignored her and read out loud:

" '. . . the Romans discovered that an evil darkness they couldn't dispel enshrouded Jorvik. They named it Nox Nucleus—the Heart of Darkness. To their dismay, they discovered that the evil, which local legends named *Garnok*, was no myth. Several suspicious deaths befell the Roman ranks. Perhaps it was the realization of what lay dormant at the heart of that evil that made the Romans leave Jorvik . . .' "

"Dark Core could be another translation for Nox Nucleus," Lisa added.

Linda nodded.

"I think Dark Core wants to ruin things for us. For anyone standing in their way, in fact. When we moved here, I figured all the talk about good and evil was nothing more than a bunch of fairy tales. But now . . . I'm not so sure. I'm starting to think there's more to those old legends than we realize."

Lisa knew exactly what she meant.

"Nice digging," she said.

"Thanks!" Linda replied, opening the package of cookies. "Here," she said and handed half of them to Lisa. "We need to feed our brains so they can keep growing and coming up with more clever hypotheses."

"Are you sure that's necessary? Because I feel like my head's about to explode," Lisa said.

Linda chewed her cookies and was just about to say something encouraging and upbeat when she lost her train of thought. She sat motionless with her hand half-raised.

"Linda?" Lisa said hesitantly. There was no answer. Linda's eyes had glazed over and she was breathing heavily.

A darkness spread through Linda. Suddenly, she was no longer in the warm club room that smelled of horses, but far out to sea. It was dark and cold. The tall waves broke and velvety blackness surrounded her. A loud roar came from deep beneath the ocean . . .

"Linda?" Lisa said again. There was a pink glow in Linda's eyes.

This time, Linda heard her. She ran her trembling hand through her hair and then let it fall into her lap. When she spoke, her voice was hollow.

"Yes," Linda said. "I am here."

"Of course you are," Lisa replied with a frown. "Where else would you be? Antarctica? Let's head over to the stable now. Meteor misses you!"

As they got up and walked out to the stable, Linda could feel the ocean's roar still vibrating inside her like a bassline. She swallowed repeatedly, blinked rapidly, and tried to calm her breathing. But the rumbling within her didn't subside until she was inside Meteor's stall, stroking his smooth, warm neck.

23

In a separate stall, Anne was prepping Concorde for the photo shoot. Derek would be there soon, and she wanted Concorde to be even more pristine than usual. She continued to groom him even though he was already immaculate. Concorde enjoyed it, though, and stood completely still. Anne didn't feel like Concorde was just a regular horse; he was unique to her, and so was their relationship. She had agreed to this photo shoot for his sake. Concorde could be a bit grumpy in his stall sometimes, when no one was watching. So it was good to get him out in public where he loved all the attention. No one, not even Herman, knew exactly how old he was, only that he and Meteor were the oldest horses at the stables.

Anne couldn't bear to think about what would happen when the day came that her faithful friend would no longer have the strength to train and compete. Granted, he was sometimes temperamental. But whenever they had an audience, he blossomed and performed far beyond her wildest wishes and expectations.

Anne sometimes thought that Concorde was an extension of herself, the only creature who really understood her. As she put her face against his soft neck, careful not to smear her makeup, she thought about the SUV the night before. How close it was. How had they escaped unscathed? She still didn't understand it all.

She tacked Concorde up and led him through the stable doors. They had time for a quick ride before Derek arrived.

As she headed off on Concorde, she noticed a pink glow in the sky. It was just above the stable roof, over by the forest where she usually rode after her dressage sessions. Could it be the Northern Lights?

The strange pink glow lingered around the stable building while Derek photographed Anne and her horse. She could already feel that these would be the best pictures ever taken of her and Concorde. She wanted to see them straight away.

Being in front of the camera helped disperse her dark thoughts—until Jessica and her horse appeared out of nowhere.

Their approach clearly made Concorde nervous. Concorde, who usually loved being in front of the camera and had been so calm, started tramping around anxiously. As Jessica dismounted her raven mount and walked toward them, Concorde shied away and reared up.

"Concorde! What's the matter? There, sweetie, there, now."

Anne tried in vain to calm her horse. The whole thing felt unfamiliar and unsettling, as though it were happening in slow motion.

She blinked, and for a second, everything turned bright pink. She blinked again, and everything returned to normal again—except she was frozen. Jessica was standing close enough for Anne to smell her shampoo. Anne clicked her tongue at Concorde, hoping he would move away from Jessica and all this strangeness. She took a firm hold of Concorde's reins and led him into the stable.

Anne heard Derek calling out after her, but he sounded remote and distant, as if there was water between them.

Concorde calmed down once he was inside his stall. Anne untacked him, figuring that Derek probably managed to get enough good pictures.

When Anne emerged from the stable, Derek and a few stable girls were peering at the digital screen on the back of Derek's camera. They seemed excited. Out of the corner of her eye, Anne noticed Jessica walking past them, in the direction of the stable.

"What are you looking at?" Anne asked. She tried to see the camera's screen over Derek's shoulder. She saw a picture of Concorde in the yard, taken as she was trying to calm him down. In the picture, he had two great, unfurled wings like that mythical horse—Pegasus, was that his name? Her mind instantly returned to the photo in the library book.

She could hear the girls around her talking about "light reflections in the lens," "dirt in the camera," "special filters," "fingers blocking the subject," and "Photoshop, you can do whatever you want these days." Her heart skipped a beat. She didn't know what to think.

Suddenly she was back again to where time was in slow motion, and the pink glow encompassed her field of vision. She wondered if she was going to faint. Through that strange haze she heard Concorde cry out for help. Then he was . . . *gone?*

Suddenly, Anne's head cleared and she raced back to the stable. Derek ran after her.

Concorde was lying on the floor of his stall, lifeless. Jessica was sitting next to him, her long legs crossed and entwined in a way that shouldn't be possible for a human being. She reminded Anne of a large poisonous spider poised to attack. The stall was so dark. It was as though Jessica had absorbed all the light.

Alarm bells went off in Anne's head.

"He's dead!" Anne screamed hysterically. Was she really too late? She bent down, opened Concorde's eyes, which seemed nonresponsive, and inhaled sharply. She put her ear to her horse's chest, expecting the worst.

"WHAT DID YOU DO?" Anne screamed at Jessica, inches from her face.

Jessica slowly got to her feet and mumbled something inaudible while backing out of the stall.

A group of curious and frightened riding students entered the stable. Lisa and Linda came running from the club room. Anne tried to wave them away as if they were flies. She wanted to be alone with Concorde now.

This is how it ends, Anne thought and collapsed on top of her horse.

24

Alex was finally allowed to leave detention. She had promised her mother she would stop by today, but that wouldn't happen now. Alex was ashamed of how long it had been since she'd seen her mother, but it couldn't be helped. She really didn't feel like going all the way to Jorvik City right now. Besides she didn't have time. She needed to get to the stable to take care of Tin-Can, make sure he was safe, and talk with the others about what they had discovered. She wanted to help her friends.

Alex smiled when she thought about her journey since she first visited Jorvik Stables. She was lost, angry at the entire world, filled with a strange restlessness that sometimes made her see red. Then she met Tin-Can. They found each other instantly.

And Herman, of course. He had been amazing.

Sometimes she wondered how many lost souls Herman had welcomed into his stables over the years, putting nervous, impatient hands to work with mucking out, grooming, feeding, and cleaning tack. Calming anxious souls with trail rides and fresh air and a never-ending supply of cookies. Alex didn't have that overwhelming sense of restlessness very often now—almost never, actually. There were always hay bales to carry, horses to stroke, and someone to gossip with.

Jorvik Stables had been exactly the place Alex needed. It may have even been her salvation.

She ambled down long and narrow cobbled streets that eventually gave way to gravel and then meadows. It was a bit of a trek to the stables, but that didn't matter. Alex had always enjoyed the walk across the fields.

She spotted a tower of blue and green metal and stopped dead. It loomed up in front of her like a giant, and she suddenly felt very small.

A deep, electric sound came rumbling out of the tower. Something took hold of her, a faint memory that floated by. Then it was gone again. She wondered where the tower had come from. Surely they couldn't pop up just like that, overnight?

About a mile away, Derek was riding his moped away from Jorvik Stables. He was going considerably slower than usual. He was still shaken by the sight of the lifeless horse in his stall. Derek had waited until the veterinarian arrived. What else was he supposed to do, just leave?

"He's unconscious," he had heard the vet say over Anne's sobs. "We need to run more tests; check his brain activity and take a few blood samples to find out more, but it doesn't look good."

"Do everything you can," Anne had pleaded.

Derek stood out in the aisle, clutching his camera, which still contained that strange picture of Concorde he'd taken. All the inexplicable things were nevertheless clearly visible in the pictures he'd managed to take before Jessica appeared. The contrast between the lifeless creature on the floor and the beautiful, majestic animal in his pictures was brutal. But there could be no doubting their quality—that much was immediately apparent. They were possibly the best photographs he had ever taken.

Suddenly, he heard a loud crash among the trees. He was so violently startled that his front wheel skidded. It was Jessica and her horse, galloping impossibly fast toward him.

Oh my god, Derek thought to himself, *can horses be that big? What is she doing?*

Derek felt panic rising inside himself like a dark, murky tide as he remembered what Jessica had been like in the stable. The triumphant look in her eyes as she stared at the lifeless horse in the stable was terrifying. Those eyes were now fixed on him, which made him realize she was in fact aiming to force him off the road. The gigantic horse was headed straight for Derek. He could feel the horse's searing heat against his leg.

He had just a moment to think, *This is going to look like an accident,* before his moped toppled sideways and he fell off.

"The camera," Jessica shouted without dismounting. "Give it to me. Now."

"Over my dead body!" Derek replied, hugging his camera bag. Jessica slid off her horse in one fluid, reptilian motion.

Then Derek heard a familiar voice.

"Get away from him before I call the police!" a winded Alex shouted. She came running up and her face was all red. Jessica took a step back. They all heard the clatter of hooves coming up the road from Jorvik Stables. It was Tin-Can, cantering toward them, unsaddled and riderless.

"You're just in time," Alex said to her horse tenderly, stroking his tousled mane.

"You're going to have to learn to behave yourself, Jessica," Alex continued, feeling cockier now that Tin-Can was by her side. "If I were you, I'd let Derek leave with his camera. Since when are you interested in photography, anyway? The only thing you're interested in is being the center of attention and making life miserable for other people. Maybe it's time you found a new hobby?"

Jessica sneered and took a step forward. For a split second, Alex was unsure of what to do next. She had no plan. All she knew was that she wasn't going to let Jessica—or Sabine, for that matter—get away again.

Alex had never shied away from a fight. At ten, she had made half the neighborhood kids run the other way by simply showing up. But this was different. It was more dangerous. She could feel it in every part of her body.

Then everything happened so quickly. Jessica grabbed Alex's arm. Hard.

They're back, she had just a second to think. *The lightning bolts. The pink glow.*

Then they washed over her. Through her. Around her.

Alex wrenched her hand free and raised it with her palm out. Tin-Can was standing next to her. The warmth of his body caused the lightning to intensify. Alex glimpsed a bluish ring of light around Tin-Can.

She aimed her palm at Jessica, like a stop signal. Just like she had done before to protect her brother.

It was happening again.

Alex immediately recognized the same sense of energy coursing through her that she had felt when she had chased after that boy who was bullying James on the football field.

Lightning exploded from Alex's palm and hit Jessica, who collapsed on the ground.

For a split second, Alex wondered if Jessica was dead, before she got up and stumbled over to her waiting horse. Then they were gone.

147

Derek got up slowly and smiled sheepishly.

"Thanks," he said. "Things were getting pretty out of hand before you showed up."

"No problem," replied Alex, who looked calmer than she felt. *How did Tin-Can know I needed him?*

"Hey. Alex."

The abrupt change in Derek's tone startled her.

"Yes?" she said.

"You're bleeding."

"What?"

"Your arm."

He pointed, and she saw it.

Alex looked at her upper arm, where Jessica had just grabbed her. She rolled up her tattered shirtsleeve. *Oh no, I really am bleeding*, she thought to herself.

"Are you okay?" Derek asked, looking worried. He looked very pale.

"I'm okay, don't worry. Just a bit of a flesh wound," she said, grinning slightly. Then she rolled her bloodied sleeve back down. "There's a first aid kit at the stables."

Derek didn't look entirely convinced. He was shifting back and forth.

"Um . . . Sorry for asking, but what did you do to her?" he asked.

Alex patted Tin-Can and took a few deep breaths before answering.

"I don't actually know," she admitted. "But whatever it was I did to her, she's gone now. Good riddance. Why did Jessica want your camera?"

"I think she wanted the photos I took of Anne's horse, Concorde . . ."

When Derek told Alex what had happened at the stable, her eyes widened.

"Jessica seems to have done something to Concorde. He's passed out in his stall. The vet and ..."

That's all Derek had time to relay. Alex and Tin-Can were already on their way to the stables.

She could tell the moment she stepped inside. The stable was unnaturally quiet.

Lisa and Linda were standing in the aisle with their heads bowed. She *knew*.

"Come with us," Linda said. Alex did as she was told.

They walked over to Concorde's stall. The door was ajar, but it was too dark to be able to see anything clearly. Eventually Alex's eyes adapted to the lack of light and she was able to make out Anne lying next to Concorde. He looked like he was sleeping. His normally gleaming coat was almost translucent.

"We can't wake him," Anne whispered with tears in her voice. "The vet's coming back tomorrow to take him away for more testing. But he's out cold. They don't know what happened. No one knows—except Jessica."

"She showed up during the photo shoot," Linda said. "She did something to Concorde after Anne put him in his stall."

"Concorde seemed afraid of Jessica and her horse," Anne added.

Lisa, who had been sitting quietly next to Anne since they entered the stable, thought back to when Starshine collapsed in the paddock.

"You know," she said slowly, "when Starshine collapsed, Sabine was there. This time it was Jessica. What if ... they're trying to get to our horses somehow?"

Lisa remembered what Herman said. There were just four Star-breeds at Jorvik Stables. Could the attacks have had something to do with that?

"It was Jessica," Anne said. "I know it was her. And I'm not going to forgive her for as long as I live."

Alex's eyes were fixed on Concorde, lying on the floor.

"Listen," she said, sounding more unsure to her friends than she had ever before. "Concorde. Is it just me, or does he look . . . *transparent?*"

"He's not turning white, is he, Anne?" Linda said, studying Concorde closely. Alex was right. He *was* looking paler, almost—yes—transparent.

"No," Anne replied quickly. "I'm pretty sure he's a silver black; he's been the same shade of gray since we bought him." She almost couldn't bear seeing her horse like this. She put her hand under Concorde's heavy head. Then she gasped. She could still see her hand.

At Dark Core's headquarters, Mr. Sands was sitting alone in his office, staring at a photograph. It was old, sepia-tone, with crumbling, curled edges. The photograph was of a horse from a different time. Its large wings were clearly visible. The magnificent animal, more mythical creature than horse, seemed to have been captured by the camera just as it was about to spread its wings and take off. Mr. Sands clutched the photograph so tightly that its edges creased, all the while muttering inaudibly.

On the large desk made of green and blue metal, the screen of his mobile phone lit up.

Missed call: Jessica.

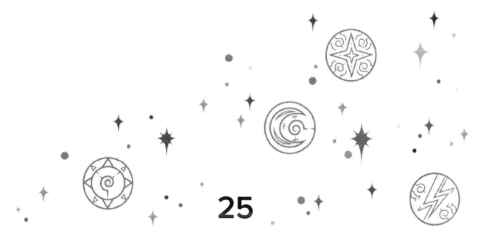

25

"Are you seeing this?" Anne said as she wiggled her fingers under Concorde's neck. She sounded both shocked and puzzled. Linda, Alex, and Lisa just stared. They could see Anne's hand through Concorde, as well.

"Ladies and Gentlemen, the amazing transparent horse!" Anne continued and let out a sort of snicker. Then she clasped her hand over her mouth and burst out crying.

"*Shock*," Linda mouthed to Lisa behind Anne's back, and dashed off to fetch her a glass of water. She realized that she was shaky herself when she handed the glass to Anne. It was as though someone had pulled back a curtain from the world she thought she knew, revealing a completely different reality behind it.

Anne drank the water in tiny sips. She seemed a bit calmer now. Alex had fetched a towel and was pressing it against the wound on her arm.

"Would you let me have a look at that?" Lisa said quietly.

Alex removed the towel and showed her the wound. Four deep cuts across her upper arm, like she'd been mauled by a bear.

"What happened?" Lisa said, visibly shocked.

Alex told them about the strange events that took place a little while ago, before she had arrived at the stable.

"To be honest, I didn't exactly relish the idea of chasing after Jessica," she said. "Seriously, should I get a tetanus shot or something?"

Somewhere within her, Lisa knew that she had to help.

Lisa took a firmer hold of the towel. She pressed it against Alex's wound and felt the familiar warmth begin to flow from her hand into Alex's arm.

She heard the melody again. It rose slowly inside her. But something was wrong. It wasn't the same as it was the last time, in the woods with Starshine.

Starshine. Of course. She needed him. The currents and eddies were much fainter than before. And this time, she realized, more currents would follow: green, pink, blue, black, pulling her in different directions. Everything seemed so confused. It was clearer when Starshine was guiding her. She tried to seize hold of the currents once more but fumbled.

She heard her friends inhale sharply.

Something black was chasing her down the stream, trying to pull her under. It was so strong. She could sense that it wanted to devour her. Her soul was literally screaming out for Starshine, but the music had to continue—*she* had to continue.

"Wow," she heard someone say, very far away.

Lisa opened her eyes. Everything had disappeared—the stream, the glow, the music. Now she saw what her friends had already witnessed. Alex's wound had healed. It wasn't pretty, but it had healed.

"It doesn't hurt anymore," Alex said in wonder.

Lisa opened her mouth to reply. Then the world went black and she felt her friends catch her as she fell.

When Lisa opened her eyes again, Linda was standing in front of her with her mouth open. She was so stunned, she couldn't get a word out.

"What did you just do, Lisa?" Alex asked.

"Yeah, what *did* I just do?" Lisa replied slowly. How was she supposed to explain something she couldn't even understand herself? "I'm not sure," she continued. "But I think I can heal people and animals who have been injured . . . Like in the woods, when Starshine was hurt."

"He was hurt?" Alex broke in.

"Yeah. He broke his leg. I fixed it."

"You . . . *fixed* it?" Linda asked.

"It starts when I hear this music," Lisa told them. "It's hard to explain. But Starshine . . . I need him. It was much harder to heal you, Alex, and I think that's because Starshine wasn't here to help."

"You're a healer, Lisa!" Alex exclaimed, her eyes beaming. "Do you get how big this is?"

"Sure," Lisa said dryly. "But that's about all I get."

"Wow," the other girls said in unison.

Linda picked some straw off of her pants.

"Remember when we talked about the legend of the Soul Riders during the Light Ride? That there are some who say the Soul Riders have special gifts."

"I think it all fits together," Alex said slowly. "I think Mr. Sands believes those stories are real. Why else would he go after the horses? And the Soul Riders . . ."

She hesitated before pressing on.

"That's *us*," she continued and looked timidly around at the others. It was as though she were standing on a frozen lake, testing the strength of the ice beneath her feet.

Linda took a step forward. Lisa followed her example, then Alex.

"Yes," Linda said. "We are the Soul Riders."

Her stomach filled with butterflies as she said it. But somehow it sounded right.

"Poor Concorde," she added.

They looked at the lifeless horse. He was much paler now, like a pencil drawing steadily being erased.

Anne suddenly turned to Lisa and grabbed her by the shoulders.

"You could help him! You can heal Concorde!" she pleaded desperately.

Lisa looked at Anne with a pained look in her eyes. She slowly took hold of Anne's shaking hands. They were ice cold.

"I thought about that. I really did. But . . . I can't."

Lisa saw the unhappy, puzzled look on Anne's face and continued.

"I can't quite explain it, but I just know that whatever is wrong with him, he doesn't need my healing. If he was injured in some way, I would certainly try to help him. I'm afraid he's simply . . . not with us. It's almost as if he's fading away."

Anne dropped to her knees, sobbing. She remembered a line from a book her mom read to her when she was little. In the book, two brothers were standing next to their dead horses. The younger brother cried and the older comforted him. *What you see over there is only their shells,* he said. *They're somewhere else now, in a better place.*

Was the same thing true of Concorde? Where was he going?

Anne thought about how she and Concorde had been able to move from one place to another in the blink of an eye. How they had evaded the SUV. Anne realized it was something beyond reason. Things like that simply can't happen.

And yet . . . it did somehow happen. This was real. Could the four of them possibly be Soul Riders?

Control, complete, move on, Anne told herself like so many times before. It was her guiding principle, which had saved her many times when things seemed overwhelming. But how do you deal with something you can't understand?

"We've all experienced something extraordinary," Linda said, almost as though she could read Anne's mind. Anne stiffened. Could she?

"Like during the Light Ride, we talked about the constellations we saw the morning Lisa came to Jorvik," Linda continued. "Could that really have been a coincidence? I don't know what it's like for you, but I *see* things."

"See things?" Alex asked.

"Yes, I have, like, visions about things that are happening. Things I can't possibly know about. Or things that are about to happen. I try to piece the images together the best I can. I think it's kind of my gift. Does that sound completely insane?"

Anne looked at Lisa, at the star-shaped birthmark on her cheek, and said, "I can move from one place to another."

The others looked at her inquiringly.

"I mean, instantaneously. Yesterday. That SUV tried to run Concorde and me over. We were right in front of it and then, the next instant, we were behind it. It was something we did, I can't explain. Just like how you were describing your healing, Lisa . . ."

Alex continued.

"And I can shoot lightning. I've known it for a while, but not exactly how or why. Tin-Can and I can do it together, and it only happens sometimes." Alex shifted uncomfortably when everyone turned to look at her. "I just did it to Jessica. When she was standing over Derek."

The others kept staring at her.

"It's so surreal. I don't know what it is. But I spoke to a woman Herman knows. Elizabeth's her name, and she knows a lot about ancient witchcraft. She says I have a power. I've tried to show her. It's hard."

"Elizabeth? I met her in the woods once, with Starshine," Lisa said. "I wonder if she knows more."

"So, what are you guys actually saying?" Anne wanted to know. "That *we're* the four magical girls? The Soul Riders? How do you figure that? You do realize how crazy that sounds, right?"

"Jorvik's a special island. Unique forces wait to be awakened here," a voice said behind them.

It was Herman. How long had he been standing there?

Herman squatted down. Resting his elbows on his knees and pressing the tips of his fingers together, he studied them gravely. The hay dust was virtually motionless in the air. Herman's voice was gentle and he spoke slowly.

"You know that as well as I do. Because, surely, you're coming to understand how certain things on this island are connected. And that you're a part of that. A big part. An important quest awaits you. In order to succeed, you have to work together. High up in the mountains, there's a place where the druids wait for the legend to come true. It's said that they are ready now."

"Quest? Druids? *What?*" they all blurted out at once.

"They're called the Keepers of Aideen and are philosophers, you might say, with a close relationship to the four elements: fire, water, air, and earth. The druids study signs in nature, in the mountains and on the ancient runestones. They live in the service of the goddess Aideen and see it as their mission to watch over and protect the nature and people of Jorvik. Some of them live among us; others have withdrawn from human society, choosing a life in seclusion. They meet in a spot they call the Secret Stone Circle. Several of my closest friends happen to be druids," Herman said and smiled.

"Before, you said the druids are ready," Lisa said. "Ready for what?"

Herman looked uncertain.

"Why don't you come with me," he said finally. "I'll make some tea and we'll have a sit-down in my office. These are heavy topics. My old grandmother used to say a cup of strong, sweet tea always helps difficult news go down. Doesn't that sound like a good idea?"

They stepped out of Concorde's stall and followed Herman to his office. Anne lingered briefly by Concorde's side. In the fading light, he looked paler than ever. She kissed his muzzle. It was ice cold.

"Don't disappear just yet, sweetheart," Anne whispered to Concorde as she closed the stall door and hurried off to catch up with the others.

26

"How much do you actually know about this?" Linda asked once they sat down in Herman's office with a small mountain of cookies on a plate between them. Three kinds: vanilla shortbread, oat biscuits, and chocolate squares. The girls dug in, famished.

"Are you a druid, too?" Lisa wanted to know.

"Not exactly," Herman said. "A kind of gatekeeper, perhaps. A sentry. There's so much that I don't know about the druids' activities. Yet I probably know more than most." He noticed their bafflement and continued with a small smile. "I understand that this is hard to take in and understand. Suddenly, old Herman turns out to be a recruiter for the druids."

"What?" Linda said.

"Huh?" said Alex.

"How?" Linda wanted to know.

Anne looked at the others without speaking. There were tears in her eyes.

"The horse matching," Lisa whispered, thinking back to the first time she met Starshine.

"Yes," Herman continued, "I help the druids locate Starbreeds, the rarest of all our horses, and riders to suit them. That's my most important task. Though lately I seem to have lost my touch."

Seeing how quickly the cookies were flying off the plate, he walked over to the little fridge and peered inside.

"Would you like some sandwiches, too? I have bread, butter and cheese, and some smoked sausage, as well. Please, help yourselves!"

Herman put the food on the table.

"Do you believe in the legend of the Soul Riders?" Lisa sipped her tea and then started to put together a sandwich.

"To be completely honest, I don't know what to believe. But I've seen some strange things over the years, let me tell you. There's something special about the girls who form bonds with their horses here on Jorvik. The girls who develop strong bonds with Starbreeds are even more special—but that's extremely rare. And by some almost impossible coincidence, here are four of you at the same stables, at the same time."

Anne leaned over the table.

"What did Jessica do to Concorde in his stall? I don't understand."

Herman shook his head slowly.

"I'm not certain, but it may be that . . . Concorde's on his way to some other place. Do you understand, Anne?"

Anne thought about Concorde's fading contours in the stable and nodded slowly.

"I think so," she replied.

"Yes," Herman continued. "Jessica and Sabine . . . they're two peas in a pod, those two. Their souls are dark. I'm scared to guess what is behind their attacks, but it's clear they want to stop you, and Sabine was able to completely bewitch me . . ."

"Dark Core," Lisa cut in. Herman's eyes met hers. She went on. "Dark Core and Mr. Sands are behind this."

"We think the people at Dark Core believe in the legends, too, and want to stop us," Linda clarified. Herman nodded slowly.

"Dark Core has Starshine," Lisa said, crossing her arms. "I'm going to get him back. Let the police think whatever they want."

"Now, you listen to me," Herman said. "Be very careful, girls. I wish I could trust the police to do their job, but all the signs point to Dark Core having infiltrated the top levels of government. That would explain why I'm not getting any answers. Starshine's fate is in your hands, but we don't really know what the best move is now. Talk to the druids. Elizabeth will help you. Trust them and no one else." He put his teacup down. "Be very careful," he reiterated. "I'm going to post a guard in the stables around the clock from now on. We have to do something to try to protect the Starbreeds we have left."

Before Anne left the stable, she stepped into Concorde's stall to take one last look at him.

"I know you're waiting for me somewhere, sweetheart," she said with tears in her eyes. "Don't worry, I'm going to help you. Wherever you're going, I'll follow."

Herman had just told them the druids were ready. Now Anne felt she was, too.

High up in the mountains, there's a place where the druids wait for the legend to come true.

Anne didn't know where that place was. But she knew she was going to find it.

27

Before the morning fog had lifted, with the residents of Jorvik still snoring in their beds, a secret meeting convened in an ancient stone structure in inhospitable terrain that usually stood empty. Many islanders were unaware of the existence of this place, but those who knew of it called it the Secret Stone Circle. There were other names, too difficult to pronounce, since they existed beyond language, time, and space. The Secret Stone Circle was an old site of worship, ritual, and magic. The place consisted of a circular, paved area where no weeds dared to grow. And yet all year round, whatever the season, there were wildflowers: red, white, and sun-yellow roses wound their way along the cliffs; cow parsley and daisies shone white.

Everything beyond the trees was shrouded in mist.

On this early morning, the Secret Stone Circle murmured and vibrated with anticipation. The stone benches began to fill with participants. They were druids, the Keepers of Aideen.

Fripp, the eternal leader of the druids, stepped forward. Though squirrel-like in appearance, he was something else entirely. His fur was blue, like Starshine's mane, and his chest white. Here and there, red runes could be seen. The little creature stepped forward and addressed the gathered druids.

"The moment we have long awaited has arrived," Fripp said. "I can see it in the alignment of the stars. Now, finally, it will come to pass. Stars, moon, sun, and lightning stand side by side and we know what must be done. We also know the forces of darkness are gathering strength. Do not let this frighten you, friends. Darkness cannot prevail while there is light. And the light shines brightly now that the fourth Soul Rider has finally arrived on our island."

"Is she really here?" asked one of the druids on the stone benches. "Truly?"

"Indeed, we have heard this one before, Fripp!" said another druid.

Fripp sighed. "Believe me," he said. "She has come. The four stand as one. Everything has been set in motion. The signs are often vague and difficult to interpret, that we know, but this time, there can be no doubt."

He looked at the druids, one by one.

"We have not assembled in a long time," he continued. "I am glad you all received my message and were able to come on such short notice. Elizabeth, would you like to say a few words?"

Elizabeth stepped forward and pushed back her gray hood.

"Over the past few weeks, I have observed our Soul Riders," she said. "Some I have been in closer contact with than others. . . . The most recent arrival seems to be far along in harnessing her power as Guardian of the Star. The healer. And there is Alex, of course. She has long been known to us. I do not believe they can sense much about their destinies yet, but I have seen their powers awaken. Now we wait for them to grow pure and strong. Meanwhile, I have seen the bonds between them strengthen."

But then she frowned.

"But we must remember that these are teenage girls, and I am concerned that they may not yet be ready. I would prefer for them to have a chance to nurture and fortify their mutual bonds for a while longer, to build their confidence . . ."

"We do not have time, Elizabeth!" Fripp interrupted impatiently. "What you say is true, but the cracks between Jorvik's reality and Pandoria's unreality are greater than ever. All of Jorvik is teetering on the brink of destruction! Before long, Garnok will break free. If that comes to pass, we will lose all that is good in this world. It must not happen. The Soul Riders must be ready now! You must gather them NOW!"

Elizabeth sighed. Her eyes were full of concern.

"Is it true the generals have already thwarted them and claimed some of the Guardians?" one of the other druids asked.

Elizabeth nodded confirmation.

"I will do my best, Fripp. I do understand the time has come and that we must hurry, but the circle is not yet complete. The Soul Riders have not fully realized their powers yet and are not ready. You know this."

"We cannot wait any longer," Fripp said. Strange galaxies and stars were reflected in his big, black eyes when he turned to the druids and said once more: "The time has come."

28

Anne had never believed in fate. Nor the goofy stories about Jorvik's history. In her family, logic and hard work were what mattered. Did fate make her mother the island's most successful businesswoman? Hardly. The same was true of Anne's dressage talent. It was all the long hours in the ring, the dull ache of sore muscles in her butt and thighs, her instructor's iron discipline, and general stubbornness that resulted in prizes and success. Nothing else.

And yet . . .

Was all that work really worth it now that she had lost Concorde?

She needed to get him back. All night, he'd been calling to her, louder and louder. Now she knew where to find him, *all* of him. Not the empty, transparent shell that was left in the stall. All that stuff about druids and magic, no matter how outlandish, had to be accepted if she ever had any hope of seeing Concorde again. She needed to fit it into a whole new worldview, and the sooner the better.

I make my own destiny, she thought as she packed a backpack full of crackers, dried fruit, water, and a sleeping pad. *And I have to do it alone.*

A persistent voice kept nagging her in the back of her head. It hadn't let up all morning. *Do you really have to do it alone?* the voice said. *Aren't there four of you? Four of you striking out together? Isn't that how it goes? Isn't that the whole point? The four of you against the world?*

But Anne didn't have time to wait for the others. She was used to taking things into her own hands.

She needed to get Concorde back, to save him from oblivion. Without him, half of her was missing. The others would have to wait. After all, she barely knew them.

Anne adjusted the straps of her backpack until it fit perfectly. Then she walked to the bus stop.

The early morning bus from Jorvik City to Jarlaheim was almost empty. She watched the sun rise over Firgrove once the bus had left Mistfall behind. She thought about how she was going to go about finding the Secret Stone Circle in the Northern Mountains, which loomed up in the distance against the dark sky.

The Secret Stone Circle? She thought about what might lay ahead as the bus rumbled down ever narrower roads. She'd never been there. And yet, somehow she knew it was where she needed to go. Herman said the druids would be waiting there and that they would help them. They were her only hope at the moment. And Concorde's. She'd ridden in the area before, but not all the way to the Circle. She was aware of treacherously winding paths that disappeared up among the highest peaks.

Once she got to the stable, Anne waved to a weary guard. She stepped into Concorde's stall. It appeared empty. The oats she left him in a gesture of childish hope the night before were untouched.

But Anne, who had already started to believe in miracles, felt she could still make out a pale gray imprint against the woodchips.

"Barely even a shadow left now," she whispered tenderly to the barely visible silver outline of a horse glittering on the floor. "I'm going to find you, angel. I know you're waiting for me and need my help. Farewell for now, until we see each other again."

She threw him a kiss and watched as her breath turned into a pink cloud just above the floor. Then she shut the stall door behind her.

Anne paused in the aisle, weighing her options. Speed or endurance? Which did she need more of right now?

Eventually, she went into Jupiter's stall. He was her favorite back when she was still a lesson rider, before Concorde came into her life. The old farm horse was once dark gray, like Concorde. Now he was as white as newly fallen snow, and he liked to take spontaneous breaks from time to time during trail rides to snatch a few mouthfuls of grass. But he was tough as old leather. Perfect for long-distance rides. Yes. It would have to be Jupiter.

He whinnied to her when she entered, as though he was expecting her and she had arrived just on time. She quickly brushed the straw off him, picked his hooves, and tacked him up. Fifteen minutes later, she was mounting up in the yard.

"To the Secret Stone Circle!" she told the horse, who immediately started walking. Before long, they were trotting.

"I'm coming, Concorde!" she whispered and urged Jupiter on.

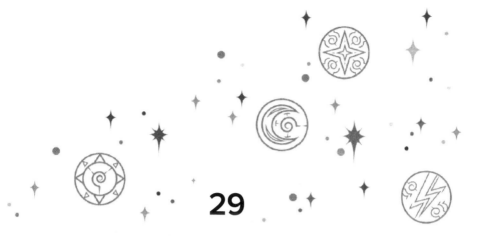

29

It felt weird to be going to school the next day, as though nothing had happened. But staying home felt even weirder. So, the girls stayed close together. However, Anne's seat was empty in history class.

"I don't blame her for wanting to be at the stables today," Linda whispered to Lisa before they opened their books.

"I know," Lisa replied. "But maybe we should text her, just in case? Ask how she's doing? I think she was going to go to the vet with Herman today."

Linda nodded. It sounded like a good idea.

"Poor Anne," Alex sighed.

All three of them were wearing big hoodies, as though they felt a need to wrap themselves in something soft against all the things in the world that chafed and hurt. Lisa missed her dad and thought it was strange that he hadn't been in touch. She tried to shrug this feeling off to the fact that he was probably really busy with some important project and tried to reassure herself that she'd hear from him soon.

"You can use the rest of the afternoon to work on your homework," their teacher said, smiling warmly. "We'll gather back here at three and go over the order for tomorrow's presentations. I hope you know your local history from Jon Jarl onward."

· ✦ ·

The table in front of Alex, Linda, and Lisa was completely covered with maps of Jorvik, open books, and candy wrappers. The library computer was bursting with multiple Google windows. On one map, the girls had drawn three big circles and several smaller ones.

"We'll set out as soon as the fall break starts in a few days." Linda pointed to the three big circles. "We have several sites to investigate, so we'll have to split up. First, there's Dark Core's mysterious industrial complex in Jorvik City. And then there's Dark Core's oil platform, which for some reason has been moored at the old wharf on Cape Point for some time now. And, last but not least, we have Pine Hill Mansion on the edge of Pine Hill Forest, where that old photo of Mr. Sands was taken. Those are the primary Dark Core complexes we know about. Starshine could be held at any of those locations." Linda wished she could be more certain, but her visions were still random and unclear.

"But we can't *know* for sure," Lisa objected. "It's simply a guess. They could have taken him to any of the old stables on Jorvik. There must be hundreds of stables on the island. Talk about looking for a needle in a haystack!"

"I know, I know," Linda sighed. "But we have to start somewhere, don't we?"

"Hey, guys," Alex said. "Aren't we starting at the wrong end? We should be contacting Elizabeth and the druids, like Herman suggested."

"First we find Starshine!" Lisa said.

"I agree," Linda added. "Lisa, you wanted to go check out the industrial complex in Jorvik City?"

"I think that would work best. I can take the bus there," Lisa said.

"Alex and I will ride north toward Winter Valley, on the other side of the Northern Mountains," Linda said. "There, we'll split up. I'll head toward Pine Hill and Alex will check out the old abandoned wharf at Cape Point."

"Aye aye, Captain Linda," Alex confirmed, doing a quick salute. "What about Anne? Shouldn't she have an assignment, too? She should come. There are four of us, right?"

"Of course!" Linda replied. "But I figured it would be hard for her to ride anyone other than Concorde. That being said, half of us have lost our horses so far."

"All right, but . . ." said Lisa, who couldn't stop thinking about her dad and Starshine. "Shouldn't we just leave now? Do we really want to wait?"

"Yes, do we?" Alex chimed in. "Come on, Linda, we're a few days away from fall break—shouldn't we be more in a hurry?"

"Whoa now, we do have a lot of schoolwork to finish before the break," Linda said in a convincing tone. "We can hold on for another day or so. As soon as school is out, we'll leave. Deal?"

"Deal," Lisa and Alex mumbled together without any real enthusiasm.

They all got up and left the library.

"Has Anne replied to any of your texts?" Lisa asked. "Because I've got nothing."

The others shook their heads.

"I'm calling Herman," Lisa said.

Herman picked up immediately. Lisa listened attentively. After hanging up, she turned to Linda and Alex. The world just became even more unsteady. She sat down on the floor in the hallway and her friends followed suit.

"What's the matter?" Linda and Alex clamored in unison.

Lisa looked pale when she answered.

"Anne's not at the stables. Herman said someone saw her ride off on Jupiter. Her parents contacted Herman because they don't know where she is . . ."

That night, Linda was trying to sleep in her bed. She'd been drifting somewhere between dreaming and being awake for a long time now. Hours, maybe. Or maybe that's just what it felt like. Sometimes, she enjoyed lucid dreaming. It was a sort of undemanding in-betweenness. She often had good ideas come to her at night, when she was halfway to sleep. The notebook in which she wrote down her thoughts was next to her on the nightstand. Sometimes she wrote poetry, sometimes diary notes, and sometimes dream interpretations.

Linda was interested in dreams and their meanings. A while ago, she had read up on dreams, and specifically about the ability to guide one's dreams. She had tested it out before by trying to force herself to dream about something in particular, but it had never worked.

Tonight, the notebook was open to a blank page. Linda was on the verge of giving up on sleep altogether when she heard angry voices. Her light was already on. She quickly got out of bed, pulled her blinds open a crack and peeked out. Were the voices coming from the street? People on their way home from a night out, perhaps?

The voices grew louder now. "The dam," they were saying. They were crying for help. She closed her eyes and saw it all play out before her.

The water, the darkness. Masses of water rushed into living rooms and garages. Families quickly packed their bags and left.

A panic-stricken horse was pulled into the churning water. Meteor? *Oh my god.* His screams were mixed with the desperate voices until everything turned into crashing waves among the ink-black night.

Linda opened her eyes, picked up her notebook and wrote. She didn't recognize her handwriting, it was so different from her normal, neat hand. But she *was* the one moving the pen. When she was done, she sat with the notebook on her lap and read the poem she had just written.

And so, so it is.
And so, so it was.

And so, so it happened
when the water rushed in
and swallowed us.

30

The house felt even bigger when Lisa was there by herself. The kitchen alone, with its big, cold surfaces, was like its own continent in the compact silence.

Anne was missing. Jupiter, too. Anne's parents had contacted the police, who had conducted a search around Jorvik Stables. Nothing. It was, they said, as though she and Jupiter had just vanished without a trace.

Lisa picked up her phone to see if her dad had called. He still hadn't, and now she was becoming even more concerned. The sandwich she had made earlier was sitting virtually untouched on the kitchen counter. Lisa threw it away.

She called her dad, but the call went straight to voicemail. She left a message while she wiped the tears that wouldn't stop falling. Tears of fury, she told herself. That felt better than tears of grief. Tears of disappointment were probably the worst. She was not going to cry any more of those.

When Lisa thought about her dad far out at sea, her skin crawled. What if something had happened to him?

The house was so dark. So lonely. Suddenly she knew she wouldn't be able to take spending another night alone.

Despite what Linda thought was the best plan, to wait for the school break, Lisa felt a greater sense of urgency. It was time for her to leave now. It wasn't a moment too soon.

Calmly and methodically, she packed a backpack with water, chips, carrots, dried meat, and an entire loaf of bread she had bought on her way home from school. She knew she'd be able to buy food in Jorvik City, which she'd get to by bus, so she tried not to go overboard with the packing. She put a flashlight in her backpack and extra batteries. Her dad's new binoculars. Two warm sweaters, underwear . . . How long was she planning to be gone? She wasn't really sure, but more than ever, she felt like she was fumbling blindly in the dark. But she also knew that she had to leave. Not when school was out in two days, as they had agreed—now.

She left a note for her dad on the kitchen table hoping that he would soon return to see it. When her phone was fully charged, she put it in her backpack and got out the map she'd already studied thoroughly. She checked the bus departure times in the app one last time and scanned the kitchen to make sure she hadn't forgotten anything. She should have texted her friends, she thought, but it could wait. Later, when she was on the bus. They didn't need to know what she was planning—yet.

She shut the front door behind her and locked it. She didn't look back.

31

It was hard for Anne to say how long she had been riding for. All she knew was that she had left concepts like time and space behind. Maybe it had just been a few hours, or maybe days.

Probably the latter: she had stopped a few times to briefly doze, eat some bread, drink a little water, and change her socks.

It had been a difficult journey. The terrain she was riding through had not seen human feet or hooves in a long time. Riding Jupiter after so long was strange, too. His movements felt unfamiliar, and he didn't react to the same commands as Concorde.

She stopped to share an apple with Jupiter and used the short break to check her phone. There was no service. It made sense—there were no cell towers this high up in the mountains. She thought about her mom and dad back in Jorvik City. They must have been worried by now. And her friends. She got a wrenching pain in her stomach when she thought about them. She should have said something. What if something happened to her or Jupiter on the way? No one would ever find them. She shuddered, then continued. It was too late for second thoughts.

Concorde, my angel, I'm going to save you. I'm on my way! she thought, urging Jupiter on. The fog was dense around both horse and rider when they trudged up the last steep slope to the place where she sensed the Secret Stone Circle might be located. It wasn't a place you'd find on an ordinary map. And yet, Anne somehow knew it wasn't much farther now.

But then Jupiter stopped.

"Go on, sweetie," Anne said, stroking her old friend. "Just a little bit farther, then you get to rest. You'll see."

She dug around the saddlebag and pulled out a carrot. He snorted happily and, after finishing the carrot, forged ahead again.

She could just about make out big boulders at the top of the slope. They seemed to glow in the sun. Everything she was journeying toward was so close now; only an old bridge separated her from her destiny.

There was just one problem, though: the bridge was broken. In the middle of the bridge, which looked to have been in a state of disrepair for decades—maybe centuries—there was a gap almost ten feet wide.

Anne felt dizzy. Was the bridge strong enough to hold her and Jupiter? If they cantered at high speed, they should be able to jump it.

Underneath the bridge . . . no, she didn't want to look down. She urged Jupiter on, clenching the reins tightly.

She thought about how she and Concorde managed to get away from the SUV in the woods. Could she do that again?

She wasn't sure, but she had to try.

Is this where it all ends? she wondered to herself. The wind whipped her cheeks. She closed her eyes and the world shimmered pink and blue behind her eyelids. Just like in the woods.

Then she felt Jupiter stretch out to jump underneath her. Time and space folded and unfolded. The moment they were soaring through the air, over the gap in the bridge, seemed to last an eternity. Anne, who had never believed in heaven, started to wonder if that was where she'd end up. Everything was so still and quiet now, her ragged breathing was the only sound.

She opened her eyes and looked down. Jupiter was calmly walking across the last part of the bridge like nothing happened. When they reached the other side, she dismounted and wrapped her arms around the horse.

"We did it, Jupiter!"

32

On the last day before the fall break, Lisa's seat was empty during first period. And then second period, too.

"Do you think she overslept?" Linda whispered to Alex in math class. Their teacher looked up and hushed them. The girls coughed discreetly and turned their attention back to algebra. Alex picked up her notepad and wrote a note to Linda.

She's not out sick, is she?

Linda kept working intently until Alex kicked her foot under the desk. She let out a small yelp and was rewarded with another stern look from their teacher. Linda shook her head irritably, picked up her pen and wrote.

We'll text her later. I'm sure it's nothing.

But seriously, where IS she? The Soul Rider thing? Do you think Elizabeth reached out to her? Alex wrote in big red block letters on the back of her notepad.

Linda started writing a response but was interrupted.

"Alex, would you please come up here and show your work for problem three?" their teacher said with a long, stern look at the girls. Alex gathered up her things and walked up to the board. The bell rang just as she was about to start writing. The rest of the class immediately started packing up their things.

"Have a lovely break, and don't forget all the fascinating things you've learned about quadratic equations!" their teacher called out after the students, who could not get out of the classroom fast enough.

Alex and Linda talked over each other as they followed the stream of students into the hallway. Their voices were drowned out by the growing excitement for fall break among the swarm of students.

"What if Dark Core has kidnapped them, too?"

"What if Jessica hurt Anne?"

"That ravine in the Northern Mountains . . ."

"Sabine . . ."

They were interrupted by their phones dinging at the same time. They read Lisa's message immediately.

Set off a bit earlier than planned. Told the school I'm sick. In position now. All's well so far. Talk tonight? :)

Lisa turned her phone off to save the battery before slipping it back into the bag sitting on the concrete next to her. She was standing at the top of an old water tower with a breathtaking view of Jorvik City. She could see straight down into Dark Core's curious industrial complex. It looked like a twisted interpretation of a fairy-tale castle, built from entangled blue and green pipes and steel girders. The area was fenced off with barbed wire. Signs on the tall fence read "NO TRESPASSING." Men in green coats were rushing this way and that inside.

She adjusted the binoculars and spotted a helipad. At that very instant, she heard the roaring sound of a helicopter overhead.

The wind howled around and whipped her hair into her face, sometimes getting in her mouth. She instinctively dove for cover and hid as best she could. The blue and green helicopter, with the Dark Core logo on its sides, descended and landed on the helipad. Moments later, a man stepped out.

She gasped.

Sands.

"Are we really doing this? For real?"

Alex was tacking up Tin-Can. She sounded hesitant. This worried Linda. It wasn't like Alex to hesitate. If even Alex, who was never afraid to jump the tallest fences, stand up to bullies, or banter with the teachers, was unsure, it *must* be a difficult journey ahead of them.

Linda sighed and put Meteor's bridle on.

"I know, it feels completely surreal. Especially now that Anne and Jupiter are missing. And Concorde. What if we disappear, too?!"

"But what choice do we really have? We have to go . . ." Alex said, adjusting Tin-Can's saddle pad.

"To be completely honest," Linda said, "I have no idea what we're going to find. But I know we have to try. At least we'll be doing the first part of the ride together."

"That's something," Alex said.

They led their horses out of the stable, tightened their girths, and adjusted their saddlebags. The low rays of the Saturday morning sun fell over the yellow stable wall, forcing them to squint. Just as they passed through the gate, Herman called out from behind them. He came running with a bag that he shoved into Linda's saddlebag.

"Some extra provisions, girls," he said. "My homemade cookies. Don't forget to eat. And ride carefully! Promise me!"

"Yes, we promise," the girls replied in unison.

"Say hi to the druids," Herman said when they mounted.

"It might be a few days before they get your message," Alex said. "We're making a few other stops along the way. First in Winter Valley, and then . . ."

"Thanks for the cookies, Herman!" Linda interjected. "Hopefully we'll see you soon."

And then they rode off.

33

The last incline seemed endless, but after Anne and Jupiter battled up the steepest part, the sun suddenly broke through the thick, iron-gray clouds and beamed down on them.

Huge, ancient oak trees towered over the stone circle like gnarled giants. Anne walked Jupiter between two stone gateposts. An old iron gate lay discarded in the grass next to it, green with rust and moss.

The tide of history, Anne thought to herself. She had always thought that was a silly expression, but now she could feel it for the first time: the ebb and flow of history all around her. *Everything's connected.*

"Welcome. Anne?"

Anne was startled and quickly turned around to look behind her. She didn't know what she expected, but not this.

"I'm Fripp."

She looked down at the creature. Astonishingly, it was talking. She had never seen anything like it before. The creature's fur was blue and shiny; its eyes were large and almost entirely black. Its tail was big and fluffy. If she had to describe it, she would have said it looked like an unusually big squirrel. Or maybe a rabbit with strange ears. She assumed, though, that it was something entirely beyond her experience.

Anne dismounted and took off her helmet. She took a long drink from her water bottle. Suddenly she had the overwhelming feeling of being part of something significant. It felt a little scary, but exciting at the same time. She squatted down to be more level with the creature.

"You're the first of the Riders to come here," Fripp said, "and I know why. Concorde needs your help. I can show you how to win back his energy and life force . . ."

Anne was buzzing with hope and anticipation as she followed Fripp. He hopped ahead of her to one of the runestones. A big rune in the middle of the stone was shaped like a sun.

"All of you—and you know who I'm referring to—have each been blessed with special powers. Yours is perhaps the strongest of them all, Anne. You can channel Pandorian energy flows and open portals."

"I'm sorry, but . . . Pandorian energy? I think you might have to explain that to me," Anne said, looking confused. She sat down on the ground and pulled off her riding boots.

"She has come here too soon," Fripp murmured to himself. He hesitated before continuing. "I understand that all of this seems strange to you. But this is where it begins. You are simply going to have to try to quickly comprehend. There is no time to waste. First you must open your mind. Shut out everything you thought you knew from before."

Cede all control, Anne thought with a shudder.

"Pandoria is a world that co-exists with ours," Fripp continued. "Pandoria's unreality seeps into our reality and vice versa. That is the essence of magic." Anne saw stars and galaxies reflected in Fripp's eyes. When he turned to her, she could see a big sun burning in his eyes. "You have to get to Pandoria. It's very important. He is waiting for you there."

"Is that where he is? Concorde?"

Fripp nodded.

"Both his body and his soul are being held captive in Pandoria by the general."

Anne pictured Concorde's empty stall and inhaled sharply.

"Fripp," she said with a frown. "I would do anything to save Concorde. But how am I supposed to get to Pandoria? And what do I do when I get there?"

"I will teach you how to open portals," Fripp replied. "In this world, you have somehow already learned to teleport, to move a short distance in the blink of an eye. Now, you need to learn how to open a portal to Pandoria. Close your eyes, please, and focus on Concorde and where he is, and we'll see how you do."

Anne did just as she was told. Time passed; minutes or maybe hours. She wasn't really sure how long it was because it was hard to tell. The runestone glowed pink. Fripp emitted a low, rumbling hum as pink light flowed through Anne's body and mind.

Suddenly, she was no longer in the Secret Stone Circle. She was soaring above a place where everything was pink and in flux. She heard a voice calling her. *Concorde.* Then she hurled back to Fripp and the stone circle. She inhaled and got to her feet. Fripp seemed to look impressed. At least Anne thought he did. She found it difficult to read his expressions.

"You learn more quickly than I expected! Now we know you can contact Concorde across the two worlds. That's necessary for your magic to work the way it is meant to. Before you transport yourself over to Pandoria, we need to practice portal opening and energy flows. Makes sense, right?"

Anne mumbled something in reply.

The air around Anne swirled with a mix of color and energy while she learned to control the energy flows and weave magical light patterns around her using her hands. She was beaming with her success. Perhaps she got a little too cocky, though, because suddenly the color splashed her face. Fripp jumped up and down with laughter while she wiped herself off with her shirtsleeve. It was streaked with color that slowly faded away.

"Nice and steady!" he said. "Shall we try opening a portal to a place you're familiar with? Stand completely still and imagine a place. Any place. A safe place. You should be able to open a crack through time and space with your mind, making it possible for you to get there. But don't disappear, just yet! You can look, but don't touch the portal until I tell you to!"

Anne thought about the lake she and Concorde liked to ride to on warm days. She usually went bareback and rode out into the water until Concorde swam off with her on his back.

"Okay," she said. "I know a place."

Anne intently focused on this place in her mind and then began to feel something stir inside her. She started moving her hands slightly and meticulously created patterns around her. Soon, a magical disc of light appeared in front of her, as tall as she was. It rotated slowly, wreathed with pink spirals.

"Try it," Fripp suggested.

Anne stuck her arm into the magical disc. Her arm instantly appeared in the air a few feet away, facing her. She waved to herself and laughed. She put her foot in, too and it appeared below her arm. Anne stepped through and then completely appeared in a different location, but it wasn't the lake.

"Hmm," Fripp said. "The teleportation seemed to work. But your actual destination was unclear. Try again."

Anne repeated the process. This time she got it right and felt a cool breeze when she put her hand through. She angled one leg inside and felt her foot step into a cold September lake. The chilly water gave her goose bumps. She leaned her upper body through, careful not to lose her footing, and saw the lake exactly as she remembered it.

Anne was awestruck. She could feel the sun's warmth reflecting off the glittering surface of the lake. But the other half of her was still standing in the stone circle with Fripp.

"Help!" she screamed. "I'm stuck! What do I do!"

"Don't panic!" Fripp called back. "Take a big step back and breathe."

She followed his direction and collapsed in front of him.

"Smooth," she mumbled.

They practiced several more times, and eventually, Anne stopped messing up. She was able to smoothly step between two alternate places.

"Bravo!" Fripp said. "Now you are ready to open a portal to Pandoria, Anne."

"But how do I get there?"

"They say the Path of the Winds leads to Pandoria," Fripp continued. "You must believe in yourself and what you have learned. Use your powers like we practiced, and you will not fail. We believe in you!"

Who is we? Anne wondered, but she had no time to think any further about that. She pulled a cracker out of her bag and quickly wolfed it down. Should she have offered Fripp one? She really was inexperienced when it came to multidimensional etiquette.

"All this teleporting and portal juggling has made me hungry," she said with a giggle at the absurdity of it all.

Fripp laughed.

"All right, so how do I get to the Path of the Winds?" she asked.

Fripp slowly turned his head to the small stone altar. It leaned out over the precipice and the narrow sliver of land that sloped down into nothingness.

Anne turned cold.

"You're kidding me, right?"

Fripp shook his head slowly.

"You have to go out there. Believe in yourself, Anne. It is the only way. The paths to Pandoria have sadly been abused and exploited. This is the only one I have left to offer. The other ways have been destroyed . . ."

Anne looked inquiringly at Fripp, but he said nothing more.

She walked up to the edge and was overcome with vertigo. All that lay beneath was a bottomless pit, an abyss. A bird flew by far below. Her stomach ached. *I can do it*, Anne told herself. *For Concorde.* And then: *It's such a long drop . . .*

Anne tried to comfort herself by thinking that she would be falling for a long time. Maybe long enough to teleport back if it didn't work out the way Fripp said it would. She had made up her mind.

Anne stroked Jupiter's nose and led him over to Fripp.

"You will make sure Herman picks him up, won't you?"

"Of course," Fripp said. "Jupiter will return to Jorvik Stables. This last bit you must travel alone. You, and only you, can rescue Concorde from Pandoria."

"Okay. So bye, then," Anne said and wondered why it felt easier to talk to a mythical creature than to her classmates. She would have to bring that up with her therapist when she came back. Or not. Anne took a few deep breaths. Fripp raised his paw in a silent farewell.

Anne took a step toward the precipice. Her heart was pounding. She gritted her teeth and turned toward the Path of the Winds. *Are you waiting for me there?*

And then it felt like she was flying.

In the western part of the Northern Mountains, not far from where they slept during the Light Ride, Linda and Alex said their goodbyes to each other. This was where they must part and go their separate ways on their individual missions. They were sad to be splitting up and gave each other a long hug before setting off.

"Talk tonight," Alex said. "And see you soon, right?"

Linda nodded, but something in her eyes made Alex's heart pang. She missed everyday life: having lunch in the school cafeteria, playing basketball with James, doing homework, and hanging at the stables. She even missed detention. At least there she was safe.

But it was too late to turn back now.

Alex clutched the reins tightly. She felt like she was about to pass out but urged Tin-Can on toward Cape Point. He studied her skeptically before obeying her command.

"Bye!" Linda called out as she turned and headed toward Pine Hill.

"Bye!" Alex called back. She wiped a stubborn tear from her cheek.

They continued calling to each other, their voices bouncing back and forth over the bushes and trees. The sound of Alex's voice grew fainter and fainter until it disappeared.

The silence that followed the last, waning echo was the scariest thing Linda had ever heard. *A person could drown in this silence,* she thought to herself. She started thinking about her favorite poems, historical battles, the multiplication table, whatever could keep her thoughts occupied. It was going to be a long journey.

Many miles away, Lisa had abandoned her lookout post at the top of the water tower and was standing outside the Dark Core facility. She had observed and mapped out the shift changes of the men and women in green coming and going. She had spent her nights at a nearby hostel. Every day, Lisa had returned to her post as soon as the sun had come up. Now it was time to act. Starshine might be in there. Mr. Sands hadn't left the place, as far as she could tell. The helicopter was still there. Lisa crept around the fence. She had earlier made a trip into Jorvik City to buy the biggest set of bolt cutters she could find.

It was time to get a look at Dark Core from the inside.

Even farther away, at a distance so great it opened up new worlds and dimensions, Anne heard Concorde calling to her. He was inside her like a glowing light. She could hear his thoughts. He was afraid, but he knew she was coming for him.

"I'm on my way!" Anne said, and this time, she knew it was true.

How many small, seemingly insignificant things had led the four Soul Riders to where they were right now? How many trail rides, evenings at the stables, jumping competitions, homework assignments, arguments, and whispered secrets? Was this what it was all leading to? Was it always going to be the four of them, even before they knew each other?

And now they were each on their own way. Soon, they would act. Separately, yet always together, the four of them. On their way to something far greater than they could possibly imagine. And they all carried each other with them along that journey.

A rumbling was heard through time and space as Anne approached Pandoria.

The time is now.

First published by Bonnier Carlsen Bokförlag, Stockholm, Sweden.
Published in the English language by agreement with Ferly.

Andrews McMeel Publishing
a division of Andrews McMeel Universal
1130 Walnut Street, Kansas City, Missouri 64106

www.andrewsmcmeel.com

20 21 22 23 24 LSC 10 9 8 7 6 5 4 3 2 1

Paperback ISBN: 978-1-5248-5532-1
Hardback ISBN: 978-1-5248-5533-8

Library of Congress Control Number: 2019955400

Made by:
LSC Communications US, LLC
Address and location of manufacturer:
2347 Kratzer Road
Harrisonburg, VA 22802
1st Printing—2/10/20

Writer: Helena Dahlgren
Synopsis and concept development: Marcus Thorell Björkäng
Language editors: Anton Klepke and Marcus Thorell Björkäng
Editor: Jean Z. Lucas
Cover design: Malin Gustavsson
Cover art: Marie Beschorner
Art Director: Spencer Williams
Production Manager: Chuck Harper
Production Editor: David Shaw

Play Star Stable and join the Soul Riders!

Start your own Soul Rider journey with Star Stable: a magical game full of horses, friendship, and adventure!

Swing by **starstable.com** and pick up a free, cuddly Starshine plushie for your in-game saddlebag, using the code **READTHEBOOK** before December 31, 2021.

Find Lisa Peterson on Spotify

Did you know you can listen to Lisa's music in real life?! Head over to her Spotify profile and dream away to the emotional songs inspired by this book, including the single "Soul Riders."